JANE

# JANE

*a novel*

## JUDY MacDONALD

ARSENAL PULP PRESS / THE MERCURY PRESS
Vancouver / Toronto

JANE

The publishers gratefully acknowledge the financial assistance of the Canada Council
for the Arts, the B.C. Arts Council, and the Ontario Arts Council, and further
acknowledge the financial support of the Government of Canada through the Book
Publishing Industry Development Program for their publishing activities.

"A Kiss to Build a Dream On" by Bert Kalmar, Harry Ruby &
Oscar Hammerstein II, © 1935 (renewed) Metro-Goldwyn-Mayer Inc.
All rights controlled by EMI Miller Catalog Inc. Used by permission.

Chapter four of *Jane* is, in the sense of a very loose homolinguistic
translation, after pages 207 to 210 of *Love's Blood*, by Clark Howard
(New York: Saint Martin's Paperbacks, 1993).
Excerpts from *Jane* appeared in *A Letter to His Ecsellency Nicky
Drumbolis from Assorted Members of the Community*
and in *Paragraph* (Fall, 1998) and *Geist* (No. 32).

Edited by Beverley Daurio
Text design by Brian Lam
Printed and bound in Canada

1 2 3 4 5   03 02 01 00 99

CANADIAN CATALOGUING IN PUBLICATION DATA:
MacDonald, Judy, 1964-
Jane
ISBN 1-55128-067-1 (Mercury Press)
ISBN 1-55152-064-8 (Arsenal Pulp Press)
I. Title.
PS8579.D645J36 1999     C813'.54     C99-930506-9
PR9199.3.M3114J36 1999

Arsenal Pulp Press, Vancouver *(www.arsenalpulp.com)*
The Mercury Press, Toronto

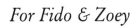

*For Fido & Zoey*

## interior decorating

I like any kind of decorative cat—stuffed, ceramic, metal. If someone were to ask me to write down my strongest feelings, I wouldn't
know where to start. They would end up sounding very Hallmark.
But that's not how I feel them.

There just aren't any words.

My favourite colour is red.

Nobody knows the anger I have inside my heart.

If I wanted to, I could be god.

# O N E

**Two girls face each other.** They're clapping, for what seems like forever. Their hands move with each letter. At first, it takes about two and a half seconds to spell out the word. Each time it's spelled out, the clapping gets faster. There are four different ways of clapping, total.

The positions are like this. First, each girl claps her hands together once. Then their arms stretch out, so the two girls slap hands, palms out. Next, each girl holds her right hand high, palm down. The left is lower, palm up. The girls' hands move to the middle. Clapping for the fourth letter is like number three, but this time the left hand is held high, the right lower.

Try to picture it—

M (1) I (2) S (3) S (4)
    I (2) S (3) S (4)
A (1) U (2) G (3) A (4).

M-I-S-S, I-S-S, A-U-G-A.

Clap-stretch-slap-slap, stretch-slap-slap, clap-stretch-slap-slap.

The game goes on until one girl gets it wrong. The two girls might start over, or one of them might want to find another kid to play with. The better girl might go for more of a challenge. The loser might have someone in mind who'll make her look good.

These girls and their friends are maybe eight years old. Almost all of them wear dresses, and a lot have butterfly clips and other stuff in their hair, which they're trying to grow longer. It's warm enough that they don't wear leotards.

Pretty soon this clapping game will be heard all over the neighbourhood, all day long—it'll be summer.

M-I-S-S, I-S-S, A-U-G-A. M-I-S-S, I-S-S, A-U-G-A. M-I-S-S, I-S-S, A-U-G-A. Their voices sing in jagged rounds, faster and faster—once one pair starts, they all get into it. They love going at it, but they're also afraid of losing. The fear gives them an edge, makes them titter and snort with high-pitched laughter at the strangest times.

The funny thing is, they probably don't really know what they're spelling. Don't know it's a place, a city, a shopping mall. Some kid some time brought the game here. But she's ancient history by now.

Chances are at least one of the girls in this playground will grow up, find herself living in a certain subdivision, will remember this day and smile to herself. Remember this time of her life and feel a little sad, like she wants it back—forgetting what made it hard, remembering only sweet moments like this one.

It takes a lot of concentration to spell and clap right, faster and faster. It's easy to become the letters and the movements and the order. It's like a drug. When we get older we can't fool around like this because we'd look like babies, which is too bad. Otherwise, we could all save some money and still have a good time.

I remember spinning around and around until I fell. Seeing the earth flying up and down, tree branches all in a crazy tangle over my head. Everyone looking like they were running sideways. I remember feeling so good, so good.

M-I-S-S, I-S-S, A-U-G-A. M-I-S-S, I-S-S, A-U-G-A. M-I-S-S, I-S-S, A-U-G-A.

Of course, there are some girls who never get it right. After a few tries, they give up, and no one bothers asking them to play again. Their hands never clap in order, or they get the letters mixed up, or both. Maybe they're trying to spell the letters out while they play, trying to figure out what it means.

No time for that.

Sometimes a girl slaps as hard as she can. It's impossible to see her do that—only the girl who gets slapped knows what's what. A girl who plays with a few kids and is hit hard each time knows she's officially in the bad books. Maybe she's got too big for her britches, and the other girls are putting her back in her place.

Teachers like to say that—big for your britches—and kids understand what it means, even if they don't know the meaning of the word "britches." Everyone knows who the best girls are, and there can only be two or three of them at a time. Still, some girls come up with the idea they're hot stuff, and start acting up. Those girls get a pretty quick reality check.

I was five years old when I said something smart to Miss Gilchrist with the class all around. I heard her say, "Young lady, you are getting too big for your bitches." I thought she was saying I was better than my friends, that I shouldn't be nice to them any more.

That was not a good thing. I already felt kind of like the odd-man-out. And for a teacher to swear that way, I knew it must be serious. I'd never heard one swear before. I did my best to be a good girl, to fit in. I tried not to get Miss Gilchrist's attention any more. I disappeared into my dress.

You look at little girls and think of how smooth their skin is, how hairless their bodies are, how fine the hair on their heads. You dream about their sing-song voices and innocent flirtatiousness. They see big boys like you and turn on the charm.

I think of the time two girls made fun of me until I had nothing to say. I remember the empty feeling when all I could do was throw myself on the ground and thrash around, like I was trying to get bugs off my skin. They were quiet until I got up. Even after, they didn't say anything for a while.

We'd been talking about how awful it would be to kiss a man's penis. I'd said it really wasn't so bad. They jumped on that, asking me how I'd know. Asking in a nasty, you-think-you-know-everything kind of way.

I didn't say anything more. Then they started making fun of me. I hit the sand around the swings in the park. Then I sort of went blank for a while.

After I got back up—as I tried walking ahead of them, away from them—they tried to catch up to me, then they fell behind, then they caught up. Just like dogs. *You're so weird, you're so weird. What's your problem. Are you a spaz?*

I didn't know how I knew. I don't know how I knew. I've changed my mind.

M-I-S-S, I-S-S, A-U-G-A. M-I-S-S, I-S-S, A-U-G-A. M-I-S-S, I-S-S, A-U-G-A.

But I can see your point. They are cute from here—safe in a car with its windows rolled down. From a distance.

## stranger than fiction

I'm good at telling stories. Telling stories is the story of my life right now. I like English and sociology. That's about it. Math sucks. Science sucks. History sucks. Geography sucks. I do okay with grades, but what's the point? Year-end exams are a couple months away, and I've been slacking off.

Next September is going to be my first year at college or university or whatever. I haven't heard back from any to know where I've been accepted. *If* I'm accepted at all. I've had to fill out all sorts of questionnaires that are supposed to help me figure out what I'm good at. To help me know what I'm supposed to be.

The job I want is to make you happy. The career I want is to create a perfect home, be perfect for you. Maybe to work with people, but does it really matter how?

All this pressure to be somebody, be somebody. Sometimes I feel like my brain is going to collapse. You would say it already has. All I want is to make you happy. My mind wanders to the thought of a ring on my finger, spreading my left hand out to show off. To finding a place where I fit in.

Nobody else looks like they want to have me. I don't know why I should think you do.

# T W O

*This is pretty much like a story I already told you—*
She thinks of stained glass in English cathedrals. Saints, children, animals, angels and blood, glowing with a crazy fury. She becomes one of the figures, feels her own skin burn. She is here, but not here.

Thom is on top of her. They lie sideways across an old-fashioned double bed with a high headboard. Thom's right hand is on her shoulder, his left behind her, squeezing her thigh up near her crotch. He pulls himself up and down.

For Eve, it's simple. Her head rests with her right cheek against the rose-coloured crocheted bedspread. She barely moves. For a while, her weak fist rested on the small of his back, close to his kidney. But with his knifing, it slowly slid off, landing slightly away from her torso.

This is Eve's first day back from a big trip. Not to England. At her grandparents' place, there was an old coffee-table book about European stained glass, full of large colour photos. When she was little, she loved to look at it. She had tried to imagine what it would be like to have others worship her, and make something so beautiful to remember her by. She had once dreamed of becoming a saint.

Eve is far away, but Thom doesn't notice. He's far away too, in a way. He thinks of feeling good, feeling skin against skin. He tries not to get caught up in all his worries. Thom clenches his teeth, makes himself think, *Good, good, good,* tries to block out anything negative.

You watch.

You got off the night bus and walked up the block, thinking about the homework you had to finish. There was a light on in a basement, and you decided to check it out. A tree nearby was the right size for you to duck under, so you wouldn't be seen by anyone who might pass.

At first, you were excited, then you got bored. Basic missionary, nothing more.

The couple is pretty young, their skin tight, which is a plus. She is about your age, nineteen. Older than you like. He's in his mid-twenties. His body isn't too big, so you get to look at her, but her doing what?

You think about what you would be doing, given half a chance.

Eve is slick with sweat and juice. The sweat is mostly Thom's. The crackling juice is hers, but she doesn't feel like it is. It comes from some place unconnected to what she feels about things. There is nothing to this sex. Instead, cathedral windows fly by. Sometimes she swoops above them and looks down. She doesn't know why she's thinking about them.

These cathedrals she thinks of as English are more like the ones she just saw in Quebec, where she went for a few weeks. On the bus, she'd seen churches that looked like they took up a quarter of the town. But she hadn't thought of the stained glass inside them. She hadn't thought of stained glass for years.

Eve had gone on the holiday alone. Thom and her family worried abut her going with no plans. She said it was the best way to brush up on her French. None of them knew there was a high-school student there.

She'd met him when he came to her school as part of an exchange program a couple of years earlier. He was younger than her, but mature-looking for his age. They'd flirted a little. They'd stayed in touch. He knew she had a serious boyfriend.

Eve only spent a few days in his town. They messed around behind his high school. It let Eve feel like she had choices. The boy seemed really proud of getting her to travel so far for him. He didn't understand.

You had hoped to see Thom's right hand move to her throat, thumb pressing down. You had hoped to see her struggle. It's been the same-old, same-old for forever, though. You wish that the basement window could be open at least, in case there is anything interesting to hear.

You start thinking about whether she has to go home after this. Whether she's going back to her mother's. You can see yourself follow her onto a bus, making the same transfers she might have to make, right up to her front door. You would follow in a way she wouldn't notice.

You find the idea of catching her right at the door of her home very exciting. Would she still be slick from him? Would she have showered before leaving? Would she want it?

Thom keeps his head above hers. His eyes are closed. He's feeling pure motion, pure motion, until she breaks his rhythm.

"Please stay still, Eve." Thom says it in a soft voice.

"Sorry, I was getting stiff." Her voice is tight.

"You *are* a stiff." He laughs a little. "And I'm stiff." While he speaks, he pushes deeper into her as if it helps make his point.

She finds the whole thing pathetic. "Fine," she says.

She wonders what turns him on about this, what bothers him about her moving around. She knows he'd never get the angle right to make her come. She also doesn't want to come. Deep down, there's something exciting for Eve, to have so much control, so much power that nobody else can see.

She has secretly started to feel she's better than Thom. Especially when she went on her trip, he seemed like a weak stranger, his phone calls so bloodless. He'd talk about stripping an old piece of furniture and getting ready for his parents to visit. Adding in a little boy's voice that he missed her.

She wonders whether Thom thinks she's better, too. She feels like she's becoming harder and stronger, while Thom's getting smaller and more ridiculous.

The thing is, when she moves around, Thom starts to worry that she only cares about making herself feel good. That it isn't really about her loving him. That all she cares about is getting off, and she is using him for it. This way he knows. He wants Eve to be happy, but he's afraid. She was so cool to him when she was away.

It's getting late, and you are starting to think you should go. She's old enough to be living with him, or to have moved out on her own. So maybe she won't be leaving. But there's something that makes you stay, something different that you can't put your finger on.

Suddenly you know. The guy stops, then pulls away from her. When he stands, you see that he's still hard. Your eyes go back to the girl. She doesn't move. He grabs her shoulder and waist to pull her over. Her head rests where it is on the bed. When you think about it, you can't remember ever seeing her move.

The guy gets back on the bed, uses his legs to push hers apart. He pulls her up by the hips and guides himself into her. She does nothing.

Everything runs through your mind again. You are sure of it, she hasn't moved. A feeling like you've never had moves in your gut. You are still horny, but you feel panic, too, a kind that makes you feel ticklish, almost like throwing up. But also really excited. All this time, you'd thought there wasn't much to see, and it's been the most incredible thing you'd seen yet.

A part of you thinks maybe you should report this. Then you start to laugh a little, biting your lip so you won't get too loud, thinking about what you could possibly say. "Excuse me, I was looking at these two having sex in a basement, then I noticed that one of them was dead, so I called."

You remember where you are—outside in your neighbourhood where anyone can hear the smallest noise, it's so quiet. Someone might want to know what's so funny. You shut up.

There really isn't much else you can do except keep watching.

The guy is obviously very excited. He keeps his hold on her hips, using them to pull her to him when he pushes forward. Her hair flares out like a halo, her face obscured. He lets go of her right hip, and uses his free hand to push hard against the small of her back up to the bottom of her shoulder blades, giving her a rough massage. Pressing her back into a curve. Then he pulls his hand away, bends forward, wraps his arms around her waist and puts his head on her back.

Thom behind her touches something deep in Eve. It's the only time he doesn't seem to be self-conscious. She likes that. When his face presses down on her back, she almost wishes she could come this way. Her hair is so sticky with sweat that it doesn't move with her heavy breathing.

Thom comes. His body falls on hers. They stay there, quietly, for a long time. She doesn't move.

You sit there waiting, then you know it's over. He gets up to turn the light off. Before he hits the switch, he looks up, right at you. Panic makes you shudder. Then you realize he's looking at the window itself, almost as if he expects a face to be pressed up against it. You're hidden by the heavy shadows of the tree.

When the light's been off for a while, you get up and brush loose grass from your pants. You press your hand against your crotch. You don't live far away. You run, the images of the night floating like a veil in front of sidewalks, fire hydrants and small, well-kept lawns.

Thom's apartment is near an air-force base, but right now Eve can't think of any time she has heard a jet go by. The only noise she remembers hearing is the shuffle of orthopaedic shoes worn by the landlady, who lives upstairs.

The two of them often joke about her shoes, but Eve actually finds the sound makes her feel less alone. She thinks about Seder, when the landlady's relatives, some from as far away as Florida, spend a few days in town. All of them seem to wear orthopaedic shoes.

19

Eve imagines walking up from Thom's apartment to the first-floor door. She would knock and be welcomed in for the meal. Almost like she's part of the family. It becomes a dream.

Thom takes more time to let himself fall asleep. He worries about where they could buy a house, and how they would pay for it. He doesn't think he's ready for marriage. He isn't sure what he wants. He feels Eve is pushing him to make decisions. He longs to go back to where he comes from, but he feels too far away now. Thom worries about getting to sleep because he has to get up early to work at a job he doesn't like.

And you. If you wanted to, you could have me be that girl lying down. I would be dead or alive. I could be the landlady or one of her relatives. You could make me your girlfriend in another town, or your mother. Or anything else.

You be the boy. I'll be a girl.

# telling stories

I like the stories in a way. I know what you want, and I say what you like, but sometimes I add things for myself. So in one way the stories have nothing to do with me, but in another way I'd have to say they've got everything to do with me.

It's weird.

Sometimes I can't believe what comes out of my head.

I'll be talking about doing things I can't imagine doing for real, telling a story where I want to do them. My girls also always like doing whatever, even if it's secretly.

Before I know it, I'm really into the story. I like that we're all having fun. It's exciting because in the stories *I* decide what I want to have happen. And *I* decide when and how things will be.

First, I think about them to myself, which is fun because I add things I'd never say to you. Sometimes I write them down with extra stuff later on. I don't show those to you, either. But when I do tell you a story, you never try to make me change it. When I'm into it, you're so busy wondering where I'm going to take you that you don't notice a lot of the details. You don't notice the little things just for me. You get so hot that it kind of slips by, which is good.

It's the one time I don't feel like a complete screw-up with you. Lately, the stories seem to be where I'm closest to really being the me I want to be! The one you love.

# THREE

**It's a hot day.** Me and Adrian stand behind the counter sweating in brown, pink and white-striped uniforms with brown bibs. Our hands are cut. Veins stand out down our arms and legs. The store is air-conditioned, but the heat outside comes in through open doors. Sweat coats our faces and trickles between our breasts. There's no way of wiping it off, not with hands coated and customers waiting.

The uniforms hide stains, but because our tops are short-sleeved, our arms to just above the elbows show every detail, every mark. Each of us has streaks of white, brown, green and other colours shooting up to the sleeve of one arm. There is also a lot of bruising.

We scoop, two ounces at a time.

Even though it's crazy busy, a third girl, dressed like us, is off to the side making ice-cream cakes. She can't help us, because she has orders to fill. Which I know is fine by her, since she'd rather not have to hustle around with stupid little cones of ice cream. Cakes and pies are more creative.

She's making Sailor Moon now, and takes care with the final touches, working quickly so the Jamoca Almond Fudge doesn't melt into the blue icing. Her back is to the customers.

One guy comes up to the glass display case and checks out the flavours.

"Can I help you?" I ask.

"You sure can."

"Yes, what would you like, sir?"

"Well, what I'd like—how you can help me—is by giving me some advice. What flavour do you recommend?" He steps back a little, like I should look him over, get to know him a bit.

I get the idea he's proud of himself. Who knows what for.

He's like most of the other people lined up past the door and along the walkway in front. He's got a lime-green polo shirt with a little doodad on it—probably some bargain his wife bought him from Zellers—and he's wearing tan pants. I think the shoes are the kind people sail in.

I'll never understand how people can wait in line for half a day and not know what they want. What are they thinking about all that time? How to save the world?

After a second, I raise my head and say, "I have a scoop for you."

Adrian grins a little, looks over, makes sure she catches my eye, and nods.

"How about Pralines 'n' Cream? It's our most popular," I say.

He looks thoughtful, a little suspicious. "What's in it again?"

I say, "Sir, I could give you a sample if you'd like. Make your decision easier." Like the guy was buying a house.

"That's a good idea." He's all enthusiastic now, puts his hands together and rubs them. Looks around to see if anyone finds him as brilliant as he does. You'd think he's never been to the store before, which I know for a fact he has been, about a million times. I get him a bit on a tiny pink spoon.

"Oh, I'll need more than that to really know," he says.

"Sure."

Once he's tasted it and decides he's willing to invest, I adjust the scoop to dock off the extra he got on the tester.

As I'm ringing in his cone, I hear some excited voices. "What's that in the ice cream?" At first, it's just a woman, then a man joins in. I look over the counter. They point to one of the tubs and stare steady at Adrian, who is kind of pale.

I give the guy his change and move in to help.

Adrian is holding her hands behind her back. She leans over and whispers, "Sorry, I'm bleeding like a pig," then goes to the back room.

Cake Lady and Sailor Moon remain calm.

I look down into the tub. There's a fine pink spray ringing the Peachy Peach Cobbler. Real quick, I take a scooper out of the warm water tray and shave the top layer. "Sometimes ice creams get mixed together," I say. Then I rush to the sink and dump the mess, rinsing off the scooper before turning back to the couple. "There, we can start fresh now. Is this the flavour you want?"

About an hour before closing, there are no customers. Because she's behind in her work, Cake Lady is still around. She gripes about a date she's supposed to go on.

"I'll die if he sees me in this get-up," she says, all huffy.

Adrian is almost hysterical—every little thing sets off a burst of crazy laughter. This isn't like her. She usually tries for the mature thing. "Oh my god, oh my god, I couldn't believe it," she says. "I'm so sorry I kept taking off so much. But, it was like, every time I put a bunch of bandages on, they'd just pop right off when I went to hold the scoop."

I say, "It was truly a day from hell. Why do people wait so long for *ice cream*?"

"The cut was in the worst place humanly possible. I kept expecting the bandages to just pop right off into the ice cream, and I'd be spurting blood? And there would be all these people waiting for us to serve them. Oh god." She's gulping air. Tears come to her eyes. "'Try our new Bloody Blood Pudding flavour,'" she says. She doubles over, holding her gut.

I say, "The way you're acting, maybe you lost *a lot* of blood. Freak."

Adrian gives me a shove.

We decide to risk it and clean up early. Cake Lady is frantic. We can

25

tell she's dying to ask us for some help. Cake Lady's date will swing by her house in about half an hour. If she's not there, he'll come to the store. She didn't bring a change of clothes. And it takes about ten minutes to walk to her house from here.

Cake Lady has a great figure but a super big butt. It gets her grief. We've heard about guys who took her out for really expensive dinners. She only gave them a tiny peck on the cheek, said thanks and went home. So she has a rep for putting a date on her ass without putting her ass out for a date.

She hasn't done the nasty.

As we're wiping down the display cases, I say, "Speaking of *banging* . . ." and sneak a sly look at the queen of cakes. I tap one of the scoopers against a metal sink as a cover. Heh heh.

Cake Lady gets the dig about being a virgin right away. She tightens up and jerks around in her seat a bit. She slaps at the icing. I've done a few cakes myself, and it *is* tricky. As the ice cream gets softer, the icing starts to slide along it rather than stick to it. Then everything starts to melt, quick. So you really have to hustle. All for a gorphy-looking cartoon that will probably make kids puke or at least have headaches.

Once I had to do one that read, "Happy B-day, Stevie." Me and Adrian had kittens over it. We would say "bidet" instead of "B-day." I walked around like a chicken, saying, "Oh, how refreshing!" every so often.

So anyway, Cake Lady is all uptight, and freaking out about the time. Her lips are kind of twitching. Me and Adrian are dancing with mops. I'm making up an opera.

"You think you're so great," Cake Lady says. The way she sounds it's like she's actually said it a few times already but we just didn't hear. "Don't think I don't know about your little codes. Don't think you're *that* smart."

Me and Adrian look at each other, but we know enough not to lose it. We just nod and keep cleaning.

"Yeah, you're right," Adrian finally says. "Sorry."

Both of us are pretty bummed out. We like our codes. For example, "I've got a scoop for you," is the worst insult. It can mean, "What are you allergic to," "Go screw yourself," "You are a pathetic idiot." But it only works if just the two of us know.

Cake Lady finishes off her last piece of art, puts it in the freezer, hops off her stool and walks to her destiny. We lock the door behind her. We pretend to take turns licking the ice cream from each other's scooping arms. I can see our enemy shaking her head as she disappears into thick night.

Once we're alone, me and Adrian stop fooling around and get down to business. We both want to get home, too.

# girly-girl

I look at Adrian and think, what would it be like, if I was a guy? Would she go for me?

I think we could have a good relationship, me and Adrian. She's been my best friend for a long time. I really understand her. I think I'd be good, in control. I don't think I'd miss being girly-girl. I don't think I'd miss waiting to see what happens. I would like to just *do* things, which is what guys do.

I don't think I'd fool around on her.

If I was a guy, I wouldn't have you, of course.

But I think if I was a guy, you might be more honest with me. We could be best buddies. We could prowl around.

I think you'd like me more.

Plus Adrian could officially choose between us, so we would finally know what's what.

# F O U R

She's about to finish work at the ice-cream store. You know that pretty soon she'll walk across the strip mall's big empty square of patchy asphalt, cross the road and make her way home through Deer Park subdivision. You wait it out in the car, which you've parked facing the store. Through the huge windows, you see her go back and forth behind the counter. You see her clean the floor.

You smoke four cigarettes very slowly.

After about forty-five minutes, she comes out alone. She locks the glass door behind her. Adrian turns and sees your car. She makes a real effort not to walk fast to you.

You say, "Hey," when she gets close enough to hear.

"Hey."

She says it as smooth as chocolate pudding.

What you don't know is she's been waiting for this to happen. She's been dreaming about it. Depending on it. It's like she's been able to smell you wanting her. And, even though she's young, she's got good enough instincts to go ahead and clear the way. In fact, last Thursday she told her mom and dad that my surprise pre-proposal party could happen any time soon. She said it would be at one of The Keg restaurants, but she didn't say which. She even talked to them about what present she should get me. Adrian said she wanted to be sure it was something you would like, too. Something practical.

"Don't be surprised when I'm late one night," she told them.

When she gets right up to the car, you say, "You gotta go back for a curfew or something?"

She blushes. She doesn't like you talking to her as if she's a kid. "No."

It's said in a hard way, trying to sound tough.

"Feel like driving around?"

"Okay." Adrian opens the car door and gets in, all easy, like nothing's really happening.

You pull onto the road, make a left to get out of town.

She knows where you're heading—to the lake, not far away. Her stomach dips. Is that it? She's thought of a lot of places with you, but never where teenagers go. Before tonight, she imagined something really sophisticated. Adrian thought about you showing her something completely new.

She's thought of a fancy hotel in Florida, or even just one of your friends' apartments somewhere in the city. She's gotten as far as dreaming of you driving up to some beautiful new house in the country, surrounded by trees. Of you turning to her and telling her this is what you've always truly wanted. That this house is for her, for the both of you. That you just want her, and to give her this kind of life. To give her what she deserves. She dreamt of you taking care of everything, making life easier.

You and Adrian hold hands lightly, barely speaking as you drive. Adrian is lost in thought. She sees the house flicker in front of her and at the same time tries to keep her feet on the ground.

There's a fake pioneer sign at the entrance to Otter Lake Park. You pull in, go along for a while, then get to the trail you want.

"Let's go down here," you say. "We can go look at the water or something."

Adrian is finally jumpy—frightened, almost. "Okay," she says, her voice high and thin. Squeaky. You are so cocky, so sure of yourself. You are my big man from downtown. You are twenty-three, and it makes her feel like a tiny little idiot.

Up until tonight, Adrian has always been in control of guys. Even the popular ones in class don't know how to act around a girl who's so smart and pretty. They haven't been near that many. They need practice getting what they want. But at this point, one wicked look usually makes them cut out doing whatever.

"How 'bout here?" You stop the car, tucking it in under some sumach. You shut off the lights and cut the engine. Leave the radio on. Turn to your right, lean over, put your arms around her.

The two of you tilt towards each other, an upside-down V over the gear shift. Adrian closes her eyes and parts her lips. She's ready for the kiss that comes. It's quick and gentle. Friendly, almost. As the two of you get more into it, your kisses grow long and deep. Lips feel bruised and puffy. It's like a pit opens up inside both of you, and each tries to swallow the other to fill it.

"We should go into the back." Your calm voice surprises her.

You and Adrian turn away from each other, move over to opposite sides, pull the door latches. Push the doors open. The two of you get out of the car, stretch and straighten your clothes without thinking. She pulls her long red hair away from her face.

When you both get in the back, without the steering wheel and stuff in the way, you ease Adrian down and undo her blouse, slipping each button through its eye without fumbling. You unfasten her bra straps, pull the bra down to her waist. She'd never thought of doing it that way.

Adrian's nipples are already hard. You lick their tips, then kiss them while you touch her face. Then you take one breast in your mouth while you caress the other. Your tongue and teeth spark small shocks in her groin and chest. She doesn't moan, but her breathing is slow and deep. She aches.

"You like that?" you ask.

33

She says, "Uh huh."

"I've got plenty of tricks up my sleeves," you say, rolling up your sleeves and laughing a little.

You push your hands under her, around her ass and up to the small of her back. You undo the button at the waist of her mini. Pull the zipper down. You hook your thumbs inside the band of Adrian's underwear and take the panties, nylons, skirt off, all at once. You take the time to put them neatly on the shelf under the back window.

You lean against the side panel as you move your hand on her crotch in little circles. After a while she watches as you move closer, your face floating out from the darkness, floating up and then down, disappearing under the crown of your thick wavy hair. She pulls away a bit when your cold lips first cut through her pubic hair. Then her breath becomes jagged and wet. She grabs your curly head.

This is the first time she has ever felt lips and tongue this way. She's not sure exactly what you're doing. It feels good, but at the same time it's like a sharp pain going through her. Your tongue runs up to her clit and down again, up and down. Your breath bursts against her heat. The weird kind of pain gets stronger, then turns into something else—suddenly Adrian's body seizes up into a tight bundle, then is unsprung. She gasps.

As you keep kissing her, she tenses again. "No," she says, pushing you from her. It's too much.

"Wasn't that good?" Your voice sounds small in the night.

"Mmm hmm."

You move away from her lap. As you take your clothes off, your hands are like the flashes of silvery fish in deep water, somehow mixed with static sparks. You spread her legs apart and lie on top of her. At first you ride against her, then you start to push in. Adrian yelps. You pull away a bit.

"I do something wrong?"

"No."

"You're so tight," you say, like you're talking about weather.

After kissing for a while, you ask, "You still got your cherry?"

"Yeah."

"Holy fuck . . . It's going to hurt at first."

"Do it," Adrian says.

"There'll be blood."

"I want to bleed."

"When I get going, I'll want to keep going. Speak now or forever hold your peace."

Adrian nods, but you can't quite make out the expression on her face. She puts her hands at the back of your neck, hanging on like a drowning girl.

"Go ahead."

She's thinking of me.

## what makes the world go around

You and me are like nothing else on earth. I am nothing without you. You don't have to tell me.

I don't talk to anyone about what happens with us. It's too private. Too special.

I read the papers. I hear what so-called friends say about people they don't really know and could never understand. Meanwhile no one can even see what's in front of their own faces, what ugly things are in their own homes. They're too afraid to really live. They're so afraid of everything. What we've got makes us different. They've got no right to judge. They live in boring houses, think identical thoughts, buy the same boring things, go to the same places. They don't have a clue there's more to life.

You know all about stupid people. And you're teaching me how to be better than them. You say trust people only so far if at all. You say don't show them everything, and only tell them what they expect to hear.

You say, "Be a winner. Live on the edge."

You say, "Normal rules are for normal people."

You're the only person I trust.

And when I look at you now, when I look at us and see things might not be perfect . . . to my mind, that's okay. Because I can also see ahead. Because I'm always thinking of what *could* be. What *will* be if I keep my focus on where I want to go.

When the going gets tough, the tough get horny.
They're so afraid of everything.
You show me the truth, and sometimes it hurts.
I'm no cry-baby. I'm a girl and everything. But I'm strong.

# F I V E

Tonight at that Tex-Mex bar—the place with chili-pepper patio lights all around—we drank with a couple of your buddies. Jim and Matty. You call them Chip 'n' Dale because they're always together, talking fast back and forth. Because they're so up on their bods, showing off in front of girls, I call them the Chippendales, but no one hears the difference.

You guys were laughing it up about some joke you'd pulled off on a high-school teacher way back.

I ordered. Usually when I'm drinking, I try to have a lot of water, but margaritas are so good that usually, before I know it, I've gone through three or four in a row, just like that. But tonight I had the water, too. Maybe I'm finally getting more mature.

I was sitting on the inside of the booth against the wall because I have little legs and don't need the room in the aisle like you do. When I needed to go, I had to say, "Sorry, sweetie." I knew it wasn't great doing that to you, but I couldn't wait. As I was getting out of the booth, the waitress came by and asked if we wanted anything. I just had enough time to order another margarita for when I got back.

So I was in the bathroom peeing, and this thing happens. I swivelled my head around to find the toilet paper. My hands were curled up, close to my chin. Out of nowhere, I was looking down at myself. And I thought, *It's like I'm a rat.*

I got out of that bathroom fast.

Back in the bar, walking to the table, I thought, *Am I ever drunk.* But I also thought, *There is something big going on.* One of those sharp, bright times where everything seems connected and clear that can also happen on a high. Where everything looks different or seems to have a new kind of meaning. I tried to get over it fast. I was scared about where my head was taking me.

When I got back to the table, you gave me a look because you were still talking, and I was interrupting again. Luckily, the waitress was right there with the drink I ordered. I asked for another one. I drank the margarita already at the table and listened to you and the Chipsters. It's funny, because right now I couldn't bet on what you were talking about, not even for a million.

There was this pet rat I had . . . I haven't thought about her for forever. Stumpy. When she was about to clean her face, her head moved side-to-side, exactly like mine was moving in that bathroom. She had her hands up, close together, curled around in the same way my hands were.

I kept Stumpy for school over the summer when I was about eight. She didn't have a tail, which is how she got her name. Me and Adrian used to sing, *Bumpy Stumpy, she's so dumpy.* There was something really cool about her. I could watch Stumpy in her big aquarium for hours. Which I did. Mom would finally tell me to go outside, and I knew I had to, because I had to keep Mom happy.

It's funny how I forgot her until there I was, heavy into margaritas, thinking I was a rat. Even then, I didn't let her in right away. She came back to me when I got home. When I started to clean my face.

A few months before school finished that year, the kids down the block—they were younger than me, I didn't really know them, they were practically babies—got some chicks for Easter. These little chicks were the cutest things.

They didn't last very long. Everyone liked seeing them run around on the lawn, yellow puffs against the unreal green of spring, making everything look bright and cheerful and alive. But it wasn't very practical. A cat caught one, the family car backed over two, and the last one was stepped on by the dad. That was the worst. They couldn't look at the squashed little body on the walkway for a couple of days, so they used the back door all the time. Then the father took the garden hose and sprayed the whole mess into a bush.

My dad said it was a stupid thing for the parents to get. He told me, *See, look, I'm just thinking of you when I say we can't get a dog or whatever.* Said he didn't want me going through that. *Animals belong in the country.*

Stumpy was snuck in. Mom knew about her. We kept her in the laundry room where there was no way Dad would find her. I begged and begged Mom until she signed the form. So as far as the school knew, I came from a family with parents who thought it was okay for kids to have something of their own to love. Normal parents.

Ah, shit, Stumpy. Why did I remember you?

Adrian usually didn't like being in my house. That summer, she came over a lot. Adrian thought that maybe she should take care of Stumpy, that we wouldn't have to be so sneaky any more. Her parents would be cool. There was no way I'd let Stumpy go, though. The teacher trusted me to do the job, which meant a lot.

What an idiot I am. I mean, why even bother trying.

My dad found Stumpy. Because he was curious about Adrian. Out of all my friends, he's always paid special attention to her. For a few weeks, he had joked, saying he wanted to know what naughty things his two girls were up to in the laundry room. He raised his eyebrows really high and gave a slow slow wink. But he must have thought it was regular girl stuff, since it took him a while before he bothered to check things out.

When he found out, late one night, Dad screamed, *What the hell is going on here?* As I swam from sleep, I knew it was Stumpy, I just knew it. My stomach tightened. I sat straight up before he'd even finished.

*A dog is bad enough. A cat is bad enough. I say no to a dog and to a cat.*

*So what's in this house? Like we live in a slum? I work all the goddamn time so we don't live in a goddamn slum. A rat! In my house!*

I could hear him stomping back and forth. I could hear my mother's slippers slap from the kitchen down to the laundry room.

When I got down there, I saw Dad grab Stumpy by what was left of her tail. Mom was whispering, her voice kind of wobbly, *Honey, calm down. Honey, could you wait just a second? Honey, it's not ours. It's not ours.* Mom's hands were out, pleading. Her head was tilted, like a dog that can't understand. She moved closer to him as she spoke. She wanted to talk Dad into letting Stumpy go, but she was afraid of getting him madder. His pants puckered open, buttoned at the top but with the zipper flying low.

Stumpy was trying to twist herself upright. She was curling herself around, wriggling like crazy, grabbing at my dad's hand. Trying to figure out what was going on. Dad shook her hard. He was pinching her tail stub to keep hold of her. He pushed past Mom to get outside.

Mom walked behind him as far as the screen door. I went past her, my voice all squeaky. *She belongs to school. Daddy, I'm sorry. Let's call Adrian. I can call Adrian. They'll take her right away. Daddy, please. Don't hurt Stumpy. I love her, Daddy.*

We were in front of the house, walking down the driveway. *Honey, you're making a scene. Stop crying. Stop crying now.* He let up for a second. Held Stumpy away from him. Turned around and looked at me. Hard. Turned away and kept walking.

I couldn't stop crying completely, but I got it down to hiccupy breathing pretty quick. My nose was bubbling, which didn't matter because it was dark so nobody could see. I licked my upper lip to catch the snot.

Dad got to the curb and walked along it till he found a sewage grate. With Stumpy high in one hand, he reached down and pulled the grate away.

Dad's bum stuck out, stuck out really high, so that the street lamp shone on it. At the same time, for like a second, the brightness also hit Stumpy. His hand swung up, and the arc made Stumpy's nose tip to the dark sky. Her teeth flashed in the pool of light. Her sweet pink hands and feet were stretched out in a crazy hope she could grab on to something solid.

Dad threw her down, just like that, into the sewer.

I didn't hear a thing.

He straightened himself. Clapped his hands together to knock off any dirt. He looked a little sad, with a small tight smile, but also like he'd won. He came over and put his arm around my shoulder. It was the same arm that had held Stumpy as if she were a disease. I tried to get away, but he wouldn't let me.

*Honey, I know this is hard. You didn't know any better. Those are very dirty animals. Dangerous animals. They don't belong in our neighbourhood, or in school.* He stopped talking and thought about what else to say. His head tipped down, then back up. *I work hard for you, sweetie.*

I kept trying to escape him. Near the end, I could tell he was pissed off. His hand gave my shoulder a sharp steady squeeze. I tried my best to stop crying. It was so hard. Especially with him hurting me.

And now all I can see are Stumpy's two little hands curled around so that she looks like she is praying. Her candy tongue darting out, licking her little hands, one at a time. Her bringing them together, rubbing them together, then wetting them again. One hand going behind one ear, then the other, then the two coming back together to get wet again. Then I see her cleaning her soft white coat. Bending and twisting so she can lick and rub everywhere.

I remember my back against the washer and dryer, with Adrian lying across from me. In the valley our bodies made, there was Stumpy. We would talk to each other about anything and pet Stumpy at the same time, long gentle strokes. We took turns holding Stumpy against our faces, rubbing ourselves against her softness. We laughed when Stumpy poked around our clothes, ran into our pockets, pulled on our hair, sniffed in our ears, tickling us with whiskers.

How could I have forgotten? How could I have forgotten?

I never asked for a pet again.

After the bar, you dropped me off. Went back to the city or out prowling around with your friends, whatever.

Mom and Dad are in bed. I'm crying like a baby. It's been hours since I came home, and I can't sleep. I wonder if Adrian remembers. All I said back then was that there had been an accident. Somehow she knew enough not to ask. She didn't come over to my house again till a couple of years ago. Even so, she usually only does when Mom and Dad are away.

It would be great just to have somebody hold me right now, but there's no one, no one.

## grammer

Adrian and I.
Adrian and I.
Adrian and I.
You and I.
You and I.
You and I.
Rules.
Rules.
Rules.

*Adrian and I are friends, but not friends.*
*You and I are lovers, but more.*

I don't want anything to get in the way of this thing that is you and me.

# S I X

Call me Keiko. Call me whatever you want.

Do you like my hair? It's long and straight, so black it glistens blue.

Until now, you haven't come to me because of my grades. You think all I do is study. But I don't need to study for school. All I need to study for is how to get you. I'm finding it hard. I'm thinking you think you don't like me. Because I'm too different. You don't want to be seen with me.

Why do you spend so much time with that ugly girl? Why are you almost engaged to her? You know, we don't have to be seen together. We can do everything inside, just the two of us. We can hide.

You say to people you think I'm boring, but I know you still think about my body, anyway. I can tell. You wonder if I would do it differently, because maybe I have different instincts. And maybe my body's built kind of different, too, so I move in special ways, feel like no one else you've ever touched or been inside.

Better.

You've seen videos with girls like me shooting ping-pong balls out of their privates.

I see your girlfriend watching me. I know she's jealous. She's got a right to be. I try to hide myself in the change room. I'm modest. But she's all eyes.

I look at her, too. Poor thing.

Now it's time for you to compare. I want to convince you that I'm not so boring. Close your eyes.

Now open them. Please, I'm shy a little. Don't touch me right away. Just look.

My breasts are so small and round. Each a sweet half-apple. So delicate. Look at my nipples, standing up like thick stems.

I'm more of a woman than your almost-fiancée. You see that the only hair I have is on my head. I believe this is how it should be. It's so clean, so pure. I'm a woman, but also a girl. She is some hairy ape, although she tries to hide it.

What do you think?

What do you want me to do? I only want to give the man I love pleasure. That's my pleasure.

You say, *Get on your knees.*

You say, *Like a dog.*

You examine me, make sure I've been patient and not a slut, like your girlfriend is. You see I'm not broken. My mother wouldn't let me play like a tomboy, she wanted to be sure I didn't break it by accident. She wouldn't let me run around wild, to get into all sorts of trouble. My mother understands it's important.

*Do you like to have your hair pulled? Answer me!*

And I say yes, because *you* are pulling my hair.

You wrap it around my throat and pull it again.

*You think you're so smart. You'll take what I give you, though, won't you? Take it!*

"It's good," I say. "It's what I deserve. You're too good to me." I've saved myself for this day. For you. You control me, and it makes me cry. It's what I've been waiting for.

*Am I the boss?*

"Yes, you are."

*I am what?* You pull again, hard.

"You are the boss. You are much better than me."

*Shut up*, you say.

*Lick my butt*, you say. You crouch down, and I do. It tastes so sweet. You ask me to put my tongue right in it, and I do.

You stand back up. You're so tall. So strong. I want to melt into a puddle and have you step in me. I want to give myself up to you.

I'm still on the floor on all fours. My hair spills over my right shoulder, becomes a pool. You step on it, pull my head back. My scalp tingles.

I feel so alive.

I hate your girlfriend for having you before me. She never deserved you. She's so dirty. But I'm glad you have so much experience. You are so manly.

You take your clothes off and sit on my back. Take my hair between your fingers.

*You're a dog*, you say. *A bitch. I like you because I know you won't say anything. I like you because I know you'll do what I want. Right?*

"Yes," I say.

You've started to move up and down on my back. I can feel your penis, that it is hard. You take my hair and wrap it around yourself.

*You're my little Chinese girl*, you say, a few times.

Then you yell a bit, and I know it's over. You get off of me.

*We'll save your cherry for another time.*

I nod yes.

*Go clean yourself up, you dirty little Chinese girl.*

I nod yes. I smile shyly.

My dream has come true.

# make believe

Shaving down there isn't so easy. It feels good right after, but then it starts to sting and breaks out in a rash overnight. I can barely sit still in class the next day. But I do it to make you happy. It's not such a big deal. And besides, other than having to shave, it can be fun to make myself look like someone else.

The first time, Mom was annoyed with the black hair dye. She relaxed when she saw that it really does wash out like I told her. But she still can't stop herself from saying my natural colour is so much nicer. Could she be any more completely out of it?

She doesn't know about the brown-tinted contacts. I paid for them myself.

It seems to take hours to get my hair straight enough. I'm sorry it doesn't go down to my waist like you want. I know you do your best to imagine it the right way.

I wish I could turn into Keiko for real when you want her. But the truth is, you'd be disappointed.

Naked, she doesn't look all that different from me.

She's not all that smart—we get about the same grades.

She curses like nobody else in class.

She's not even really Chinese.

Plus, she smokes. I guess you've never seen her smoke. I know if you ever did, you'd totally lose interest.

*Like kissing an ashtray.*

It's okay for guys to smoke, but girls smell funky to start with, so they don't need any help.

And if you found out she isn't a virgin, you'd say it'd be like fucking a toilet bowl. She'd be stretched out of shape, "broken in," which equals broken down.

If you don't find out about her soon, then maybe at least you'll move on to someone else. She just takes so much work, and I've got other things I'd rather do with my time. I want you to be happy, especially because you don't seem to be, lately. It's like the harder I try, the worse things get.

# SEVEN

**You talk to your buddies about how good I am at it,**
saying that you're training me to do exactly what you want. There is
only a bit of coughing in the living room after you've been going on
for a while. Then I hear your snorty little laugh. Finally, you say,
"Come on, guys, snap out of it."

I don't know where you pick things up. You get them in your head
and you're like a broken record. Usually, I just hope you'll get over
your fixations. But this time, I'm getting to where I miss that wham-
bam jag you were on. I miss when all I had to do was tell you my sexy
stories. My jaw aches. My lips would be really chapped by now if I
didn't use tons of Vaseline.

You ask me if I like it. I tell you yes, I love it, I love you. What am I
supposed to say? You look down at me. All cool. You never bend at
your knees, pull me up to stand in front of you, kiss me on the lips . . .
like you did before, when I first gave it to you.

"We're past that," you say. "Relationships change."

How do I convince you that the way we were is better? I mean, it's
so obvious. But I know to let time tell.

I wait a few minutes before coming through the swinging door
from the kitchen with the mini-pizzas. All the guys have their eyes
down—looking at their hands, the floor. They're all so big on the
chairs and the couch, filling up the living room. It looks like a doll-
house room with them in it.

I'm careful to go over to you first. You take a mini-pizza. It's too hot, making your hand jerk. You put the pizza into your mouth fast, like you can't think of where else to put it. Like you're on auto-pilot. Your face screws up as you chew. You grab a napkin from the tray I hold, spit the pizza into it.

"Tastes like shit," you say, then make that laugh again. You throw the napkin back on the tray. "When exactly are you going to learn how to cook like your mom? You gotta know I'm not marrying you till then." You look around the room.

The other guys laugh.

I know enough to say sorry and move on.

The guys take their pizzas. Some almost whisper how they think the food is good. I don't look at them, just get out as soon as possible. I mean it's only pizza. And it even came from a package—all I did was heat it up. We've had these mini-pizzas before. But for some reason, today is different. I've failed some kind of test.

Will I ever get it right?

You come into the kitchen and give me hell for making the guys sorry for me by being all pouty. You lock the door, push my head down so I have to get on my knees. I know what is coming.

"Practice makes perfect," you say. Your eyes focus on the microwave. You don't seem to blink.


Do you remember when I danced the first night? When I was just wild for that song, moving around, my four fingers up in the air? You said I was biting my lower lip and it really turned you on. You said that the way I had my arms up, the way I had my fingers out, it was like I was totally saying bullshit to everyone.

You said you liked that, too.

You came over and danced close to me. I noticed right away. I couldn't believe how you looked. It was so perfect.

I had just started grade ten a couple of months before. You were so mature and different from the geeky guys in school. Your clothes were so sharp. You were like an impossible mix of Brad Pitt in *Interview with the Vampire* and a preppy Kurt Cobain. Nice jacket and pants, but with a T-shirt. Hair short on the sides, longer and a little curly on top. Bright white smile.

You started to touch me while we danced. Everything was just sound and movement. It was right in me. It felt so good.

The first thing you said to me was, "I can't believe it."

I opened my eyes and looked at you.

"I can't believe it," you said again. You were smiling that beautiful smile. Looked me up and down. "You just keep going. You're Everready. You're a bunny. It's incredible." The flat of your hand glided down my abdomen, cupped my crotch. You squeezed.

"I'd like to try tiring this out some time," you said. "Bet I could."

I laughed and maybe pulled away a bit. You made me self-conscious, excited. My mind felt lighter. I couldn't believe my luck. I couldn't think of a thing to say.

"Don't be shy," you said, then pulled me tight to you.

The next day you sent a dozen long-stemmed roses. They were pink.

It was fate, I know it was fate, and I don't want to fight it. I knew that night I would do anything for you. I knew then that it was all for better or worse.

Even now that things aren't so perfect, that I keep screwing up, my friends tell me how great-looking you are, that you're such a catch and I'm so lucky. Mom and Dad are so glad I've got someone stable, with a future. They've relaxed—they don't feel a need to watch me like a criminal any more. They know I'm taken care of. I'm spoken for.

Not that their watching ever kept me from anything. And anyway, how would it help when the biggest problem in my life is them?

There are two shelves in my room where all the little presents you used to bring are almost falling off, there are so many. Sometimes I put on one of the nighties you bought. I lie in bed and listen to music on the walkman. My eyes are closed and I'm thinking about the first time we kissed.

Sometimes I come out of feeling this way, and there's a little pile of hair on my pillow. I've also been sucking my thumb. I'm sort of aware that I do it, and I know it's a bad habit, but it helps me get to where I want to go to feel good again.

It's not like I'm making any bald patches or anything. It's not like I'm going to need braces. It's no big deal. But what a loser, pulling my hair out over a pretend kiss.

# margaritaville

Getting drunk is so stupid, but it can be so great, too. Sometimes I can't believe the things I do when I've been drinking.

What happens is I get a nice buzz. But nine times out of ten by that time I've already drunk way more than I needed to get the buzz. So I'm feeling all nice and warm, everything's just fine, and then the other drinks kick in.

Sometimes, I find myself caught up in some pretty dark thoughts and dark feelings. I get on some nightmare version of the Cyclone, and I'm spinning round and round and the floor disappears. Scary old things start dropping on top of me.

I get back into drinking, fast. This time, not to feel good. This time, to try to get rid of the dark stuff.

It's scary but kind of exciting, too. All this stuff bubbling up, about to swallow me, but then I get back in control by going completely out of control.

Sometimes, I don't remember what happened. A wicked hangover the next day tells me I could have done anything. I know there had to be some reason for me to get that drunk. Maybe I don't know what I did after a certain point, and that's a little weird, but I also don't know what was coming into my head, and that's good.

I don't want to know. I would rather have it stay somewhere else, in some murky swamp in my brain. It's like the Creature from the Black Lagoon, waiting in a dark wet corner to pull me down.

# E I G H T

**Say I'm seven.** Adrian is fifteen and my babysitter.

You are the age you are now, twenty-three.

My parents have gone out for the night. They're at the social club. They promise to be back by one. They know how strict Adrian's parents are.

It's now eight-thirty. Almost bedtime for me.

Adrian looks like she looked when she was fifteen, when you first met her a couple of years ago, only better. She's wearing cute little tennis shorts, a light green tank-top and her hair in a ponytail held by a forest-green scrunchy. She's got a miniature plastic soother around her neck. It's hot pink. She has no shoes or socks on. The skin on her legs is smooth and tanned.

I look like I looked in grade three, only my hair is more blonde and longer. Try to remember that school picture I showed you of me smiling like a little girl, my red cheeks brought out by the rose-coloured dress with white stitching. Tonight Adrian has brushed out my hair, which falls to my waist. I'm wearing a cream-coloured teddy with eyelet trim around the arms and neck, as well as on the panties. The pattern is of teddy bears and rocking horses, with a few red hearts sprinkled around.

You're perfect, as usual. But you're not on the scene yet, so Adrian and I aren't really thinking about how perfect you are.

Neither of us knows you, although we've seen you around and

both of us have secret crushes on you. Adrian already thinks of you when she kisses her pillow for practice. I imagine you holding my hand and taking me to fun places. Sometimes I get to sleep that way, grabbing on to one of my stuffed toys. Sucking my thumb, which I know I'm too old for.

Even though I'm eight, I'm very experienced, sexually. Somehow I just know things. It's natural to me. I like girls as much as boys. I even seduced Adrian a few times when she babysat. Once, I snuck my finger into her. She got angry. She's saving herself, and takes it very seriously.

I told her it was an accident. I cried. She believed me after a while.

Tonight we're playing strip tag. When the person who's It touches the person who is not It, the person who isn't It has to take something off. We've both been caught once. That's why we're barefoot.

We are laughing and laughing. My hair is getting into a crazy loose tangle. Adrian's red ponytail bounces around. Her breasts move tightly under her tank-top as she runs. I'm about to get her again when we notice something move slightly from behind the mud-room door.

Then we can't see anything, so it could be that our imagination was playing tricks on us in the first place. We're caught up in our game—we don't worry too much. We look at each other and laugh about being scaredy-cats, then start to run.

I touch Adrian. She starts to pull her ponytail out, claiming the scrunchy counts. I pout and say no fair. She takes her tank-top off. I sneakily squeeze one of her breasts. She slaps me away, giggling.

This is when you come out from behind the door.

We recognize you, and we blush. I cling to Adrian's side. We're scared, but it's like our dreams have come to life, too.

You seem nervous and sure of yourself at the same time. Your breathing is a little heavy—you've been watching us play. You keep looking at Adrian's breasts, softly licking your lips. Your feet are spread apart, and you shift from one to the other. I think of a cat.

The knife is in your right hand, ready.

You clear your throat to say, "Do what I want, and no one gets hurt."

Adrian and I squeeze each other. We move closer together. I want the knife to come out of your hand. I want my hand in its place. Adrian pulls away from me a bit, suddenly thinking about her breasts. She crosses her arms. She is biting her lips, which looks pretty.

I bite the nails on my left hand. It's a nasty habit.

"You'll do what I want," you say again.

"Do what I want!" But you don't explain. This is getting too scary. More time goes by with all three of us frozen.

"What are you, deaf? Do what I want." You point with your knife, waving from Adrian to me. You clear your throat. "Keep going," you say.

"You want us to play tag?" I try my best little-miss-mouse voice, but it comes out kind of rough. Tomboy.

You look at Adrian. "No, keep going. You know what I mean."

You're thinking about how I touched her titty. You look at Adrian because she's much older. You have no way of knowing I'm actually better at playing. That I'm the one who gets what you mean.

Adrian stands there, stupid with fear. I throw myself against her. You are almost as surprised as she is. My arms reach around her waist. I cry a little play cry, and she lets her hand fall to my back, between my shoulders. I quiet down.

I push my face into her. I breathe deeply. I can smell her fresh cotton panties and feel her pubic hair push like gentle springs against my head. I nuzzle her, nose against crotch.

It's as if she's been jolted from a trance. She gasps and her body snaps alive. "No," she says. Adrian grabs my cheeks and shoves me away. I stumble backwards, hitting the wall. My head hurts.

"Adrian, you shouldn't do that. I did what he asked." I'm crying for real. "We're in trouble now."

We both look over to you. We expect you to be very angry, but you aren't. The knife is loose in your hand. You laugh a little, walk over to me and tug a piece of my hair.

"You're a frisky one, aren't you?"

I blush.

"How did you learn to be so naughty?"

I blush harder, but I'm also sort of mad. "I'm not naughty. You scared us and asked us to do something. I was trying."

"Oh, you're good, all right."

You pat me on the bum.

"Let's go upstairs," you say. You have to take Adrian's arm and keep hold of it as you shove her from behind. I am last, my head bent and my pointer finger curled into my mouth. At the landing, you and Adrian turn to walk up the last few stairs. The light on Adrian's breasts is very beautiful.

# careful

When I'm with you, I think only of you. When I am alone, I think of you.

I have a mother, a father. I was a surprise baby, a miracle. My parents used to tell me all the time it was a long, hard labour. They used to say it was worth it. Mom would go into all sorts of details about the pain I caused her right off the bat. How it was all so unexpected. I have an older brother and sister, Thom and Eve, who don't visit. We don't have much in common anyway. It's like I'm an only child.

My parents are semi-retired. They spend most of the winter travelling. They worry all of the time about money. I stay at home. I don't get into any kind of trouble they can really see, so they figure everything must be okay. Even when they're home, there's a lot I get away with.

Because I'm careful.

It's like I'm an orphan. That's one of the things you like.

"I've got you all to myself," you say.

# NINE

Adrian asks me what I'm doing with you. She tells me how she would never let herself be treated the way I let you treat me. How you're worse than my dad. It's all easy for her to say—she's never officially been tested. I don't even know if she could ever fall in love. She's selfish. And she definitely has no idea how it can feel with you, even though sometimes you hint that something might be going on between you.

Adrian spends too much time in her head. If it weren't for her looks, she would be such a loser. She never lets go. She never has fun. She doesn't even buy great clothes. But the hair and the body and legs let her get away with murder. She can be such a bitch. And she's obviously so jealous. It's pathetic.

I never thought I'd feel this way about her. I thought she was different. But she's a girl, no two ways about it. I have got to watch my back.

All those fresh-faced young men you hang around with. All so marriageable-looking, and at the same time so wild. Which makes them even more sexy. (I'd never tell you that!!) Adrian doesn't seem too interested in them, which I can never get over. But it turns out to be a good thing, anyway. It would be a guaranteed disaster if I ever tried to set her up with any of them, much as I want to get her out of circulation.

Every time I see some of your boys, they're either on the prowl or with new girlfriends. I hardly ever see the same girl twice. And if I do, she's with a different guy. Your buddies trade them as easy as hockey cards. I am the exception to the rule. None of your buddies would even think about trying to pick me up or flirt.

How did we luck out by finding each other? We're so perfect together. No, you're so perfect. And somehow I've cast a spell on you. I'll do everything I can to help you get as far as you deserve, which is very far. I'll do everything I can (which is equal to nothing—hah!).

I look at Adrian, saying these horrible things about you to me, and all I can think is, what a cock-tease. And the way she goes on and on about what she's going to study, where she's going to go after finishing high school—you'd think there was no one else in the world with important plans to make.

I mean, I'm hoping to get *married*. Meanwhile, she barely even talks about guys. Maybe she's a lesbian.

So I finally say something about it, about how one-sided everything is, how she talks about herself, and she turns around and asks me who I'm kidding.

"You're not even engaged yet, and you're not going to be any time soon. Not to him."

"Fuck off," I say. "What do you know?"

"I know he's a snotty jerk and you could do way better. He's using you. I know you're too smart to spend all your time thinking about a stupid dress you'll wear for one day, just to be stuck with that idiot."

Adrian gets up and starts walking. I watch her. Then she turns around and says, "One-sided? You think I care about matching parasols and whether bridesmaids should have frills or lace on their shoulders? That's all I've heard from you for the last two years. That and how your boyfriend's so wonderful. Like shit. I've had it."

I have to stop myself from hitting her. It's as if time has stopped. It's as if Adrian has a halo—some weird glowing light around her in yellows and blues. It seems to be showing me exactly where I should grab her. Part of me measures everything out. I see myself grab her head. Hook my leg around hers and push her back. I see her lose her balance while I keep hold of her hair. I feel my hands pound her head into the school floor over and over again. I feel really warm inside, a good kind of warm. But it's just when my muscles tense and I start to go for her—I didn't *decide* to do this, I'm just doing it—that she turns away, throwing me off.

It takes some work to shake out of my zone.

She turns around and, as if I care, she walks out of my life. But no, that's wishful thinking. She's out there somewhere, plotting. Plus, I have to see her at school and work. And you'll be asking what's up with her. You'll blame me for everything, tell me I'm a fuck-up.

Which is exactly what she wants.

How could I ever have thought of her as my best friend? My only real girl friend. She says she doesn't like you so she can get me off guard. You've told me some of the things she's done when I'm not around. You've told me how you can tell she wants you. That she gives you all these signs. And maybe even more than that.

I'll give her a call a little later on tonight, before you phone. I'll tell her I'm sorry. For now, I'm going to have to make an effort not to talk so much about you or us or my dreams. I'll do everything I can to make her feel close to me again.

Anyway, the school year's almost over, and it would be a hassle to try to figure out who else I could hang out with. I guess it was stupid of me to think she should be any different than the others. She is just another girl. I'll have to keep that in mind. And even with what's happened, I do still like her.

Things will be okay.

# aliens

Mom seems to be in bed almost all the time. She cries and cries. She says she can't take it any more. Can't take what? I'm the one who keeps the house clean. I'll admit, she still cooks holiday dinners. She's good at it. All Hail Mom, the Great Cook.

But even then, most of the time she can't hold out long enough to actually sit and eat with us. Just before the timer goes off for the final dish, it's like her brain implodes. She blathers and spits, and that's all she wrote. It's always guaranteed to be a very special occasion.

I don't mind when she's not around. Her breath is like poison. There's this sour acid smell that comes off her skin. She can never seem to get clean. It's like she's decomposing right in front of us.

Dad barely talks to me any more. He's like some alien lurking around. With you he might talk about sports or ask you downstairs to the bar for a drink. Who knows what you two talk about then. Neither of you spills the beans to me. I hear you guys laughing. You're the son he never had, even though he had a son.

Before I met you, when I was just growing out of being a kid, I'd catch Dad looking at me all weird when he thought I couldn't see. It bugged me. Sometimes I still catch him, but not as often. It doesn't bug me as much. I guess I'm used to it.

Up until I was eleven, Dad and I used to go tobogganing down the hill at the back of the house. He used to sit behind me, holding me tight. But now he doesn't know what to do, so he doesn't do a thing.

Except maybe criticize. He's a prizewinner at that. I'll admit he's re-laxed since I snagged you, but I can tell he's waiting for me to screw this up, too, so he can say he told me so.

Dad's always wanting me to be more like a lady. He's worried maybe that I'm a slut. I've always wished he'd be more like a real man. That he'd take care of me and Mom the way he's supposed to. That maybe Mom would get better if he could just do that. But do you see me telling him off?

Even you are this bossy guy I hardly know. When we go dancing, I see you laugh and joke with other girls, but it's *Do-this, Do-that, Get-away-from-me-now* with me. It's, *Why-didn't-you-save-yourself-for-me?* Like I wasn't supposed to do anything before I met you. Like I always had a choice.

# T E N

*You can cut my hair.*

"Keiko," you say. "Bad dog. You've been a slut in heat."

"No," I say. "I've been good. I wait only for you."

"Liar," you say, and hit me. Not hard. You pull my head back and hack off another chunk of black hair.

You say, "I want to hurt you, but you like it when I hurt you. It's hard to think of how to hurt you so it really hurts."

"Do anything," I say. "I deserve anything you do to me."

I say, "I don't deserve you."

By now I have rough bangs, and a couple of handfuls of hair near the back of my neck are gone. It took so long to grow my bangs out. I'm a little sad, but I try not to show it. You're not interested in sad.

"I am your dog. Your bitch."

"You're a bitch in heat. Don't think I didn't see you with that Randy guy at school."

*Shit, what's with this "Randy guy"?*

"Answer me!" You pull my hair back again, only this time it's to grab my throat and squeeze. You still sit on my back. I gag, collapse on the plush ivory carpeting. Curl up like a baby before it's born.

You are shaking me by the throat. I need to breathe.

"You'll do anything for me? But you can't wait to get it, so you do it with any fucking little wienie bastard. Fucking right you don't deserve me, bitch." You bend over and bite my breast.

"Please," I try to say. My tongue is getting thick in my mouth. I see black and purple spots.

There is the sound of a door downstairs. You let go.

"What are we having for supper?"

You say it, almost like you are in a trance, your voice coming from another place. I hear my father downstairs, his question echoing your own.

"Mushroom chicken," I say, but it doesn't come out. My throat is so sore.

I am dizzy. My ears are ringing. I notice the deep marks near my nipple where you bit me. Luckily, you didn't break the skin.

"Chicken," you say so my father can hear.

That's the problem with girls. They seem so boring and predictable. I start to think there's nothing about them, no need to pay attention. But there's always the chance something is happening behind the scenes that I don't know about. They're sneaky.

I screwed up, and I paid for it. I'll have to know more about what's going on with whichever girl I am supposed to be before I play her.

I am so mad at Keiko. What was she doing fooling around with someone right out where you could see? Someone I couldn't ever even guess about. I mean, *Randy*? You were right to call her what you did. You must be so disappointed. If only she knew how you felt, how you watched her, maybe this wouldn't have happened. What a drag.

It's so sad that it takes a while for my hair colour to come back. I'd do anything to make you feel better, but that'll be hard as long as I look a little like her. I've got to say that, for me, the bright side is, I won't have to go through the hassle of being her again.

My sweet baby, I'm so sorry.

# practice makes perfect

Supercalifrajalistic expialedotious,
how I seem to feel these days
is really quite atrocious

School is almost over, but it seems like it'll never finish. Days just drag and drag. It's been almost my whole life. It's been pretty well all I can remember. What will the world after school be like? A never-ending summer holiday?

The thing about summer is, I look forward to it so much, then the school bell rings for the last time, and I'm out. Year after year, it seems like I run from school all excited, and then it sinks in that I'm going to have to fill time for two whole months. I barely get to enjoy the freedom before boredom and nothingness swallow me up.

Last summer I worked, and felt so alone because you weren't there with me all the time. It was just ice cream, aching muscles, and trips to malls. Is that what the rest of my life is going to be? Nowadays, I can't wait to see you, and then when I finally do, it's like you don't want to be with me. You want to be with one of the other girls.

Why do you hate me so much? Why do I love you so much? Why can't we just get a nice house and settle down? I'm sure things would be different. I'm sure the problem is that we spend too much time apart.

# E L E V E N

Last night you slept over. Most of the time in my room. It's so weird how quiet we can be. It's fun. We wait till Mom and Dad are asleep, then you sneak off the pull-out couch up to my room. You go back just before it gets light.

This morning, you were already sitting at the kitchen table when I got up. Your hair was a bit crazy at the back, and you had a funny cowlick through your bangs. The whole thing was just so cute I couldn't get over it. Under the table, I rubbed my foot up and down your leg. We had Honey Nut Cheerios. I cut a big fat strawberry and put it on top of your cereal. It was supposed to be like my heart.

We were getting ready for a special weekend trip.

To tell the truth, I hate visiting your parents. It's as if they think I might be dragging you down, taking you away from concentrating on your priorities. As if I'm not a big part of your future. For whatever reason, they don't want to think of me as their daughter-in-law. Well, I don't like the picture of them as my in-laws, either.

I've seen your parents maybe five times. I saw your sisters only once, at Christmas the first year we were together. Last year, you came to my place for the holidays. You said the food was better and my parents are easier to live with. Your mother's such a bitch, but mine is just a loser. I can't comprehend how something as amazing as you came out of that house.

After breakfast, we each showered, then dressed, and now we're on the road. It's kind of miserable because you don't have air conditioning. The sun is bright and hard, even though it's only nine-thirty, but we have to keep the windows up so the car can go faster and not use up so much gas. I don't really understand this kind of stuff. But then that's no surprise.

You love being in your car. You even like it when it's so hot. You are curled up, driving. You keep one hand on the gear shift, except on the highway. You feel safe. You used to say that you sometimes felt like an astronaut, exploring the unknown from the safety of your spaceship. You float when you're driving around. You can disappear into the scenery, check things out.

I think you get a bit territorial when I'm in the car very long, as if no one else should think they've got a right to be here. Like there's only room for one, with maybe a visitor every once in a while. Like I'm using up your precious oxygen.

You keep that car so clean. There's not a dent in it. There is a scratch, though. You won't tell me how it got there a couple of months ago. The one time I asked, you freaked right out. You yelled, *None of your business.*

We're going down the highway. The radio is pretty loud. You're drumming your thumbs against the steering wheel. You're chewing your lip. I watch the side of your face, look out for roadkill. It's so sad to see all those raccoons. Sometimes a little gopher or even a porcupine. But the worst is when it's a dog or cat.

I remember one time seeing a dog running in circles on a median between two expressways. There were off-ramps throwing crazy shadows over everything, and an old old cemetery nearby, crowded in by the roads. This dog ran to the edges of the raggedy brown grass, turning around, looking. It didn't seem to bark. We just whizzed by, but the picture stuck in my head. It's like I saw it there for hours, waiting for its family to come and take it back. The dog would starve, or try to bolt across the road and find its way back home, only to be hit by a truck or van.

It was hard not to cry.

You look straight at the road, but your mind is somewhere else. The speakers in the back of the car are a little loose. When a song with a lot of bass comes on, there's a rattling noise. I hear the pounding in my heart. I watch you. After a while, you say, "What the fuck are you looking at?" You don't move your eyes or anything.

Half the time, I don't even want to guess what's going on in your head. Used to be I thought we were totally connected, that we totally understood each other. Not any more.

I think I fall asleep.

In your beautiful car with its mysterious scratch, I fall asleep. The sun sits on my head and I feel a crusty sweat under my arms. Not very lady-like. My head rests against the window. Sometimes, when you brake or turn, I feel a sharp jab against the pane. I see dead dogs with their tongues sticking out of their mouths. I lick icing off a knife. I am swallowed by the sun, spinning above the car, flying over the fields around us. I'm part of a music video for a song on the radio. I am loved, famous, understood.

I feel a sludgy drool coming from the right corner of my mouth and know I am awake. It's trailed onto my shirt. It's left a bit of a smudge on my face. I don't think you can see this (even if you *did* bother to look over at me). I rub the side of my face against the car seat.

That's when I realize I don't have a clue where we are.

"What's up, hon?"

You don't look at me. You say, "Shut up."

I have the sick feeling. I know the worst thing I can do is get all spinny and start to beg. I know that, whatever I've done, I just have to accept what's coming. That makes it easier. You are harder on me when I beg.

There's no sense in asking myself what it could be, but I can't help it.

I take out my compact, bring the mirror up close and look, section by section. I see little flecks of skin, blotchy colouring, small bumps, shadows under my eyes, even creases. I am getting old so fast. It's really not fair that I've got wrinkles when my cheeks are still full of baby fat.

I run my nails across the skin to get rid of whatever can come off. Get out some cover-up and go to work. Finish with powder. I do my best. It's depressing, how flawed I am.

Maybe I can catch this on time, turn myself around, calm you. But it's hopeless. I know the bigger problem is inside of me, is between us. You and I. It's something deeper. Something I can't get close to. I'll do what I can with what's on top, though. I work on my eyes, then close them and pretend to have gone to sleep again.

My mind is counting every way I've ever failed. I see myself in little dresses and party shoes. Grown-ups said I was a pretty girl. But I was never very popular. I've always felt like some people can see inside me. Like I'm a freak. Like there was something I needed to hide.

Even now, I feel safer around older people. I don't do as well in school as I should. My friends can't really count on me. I think too much about myself.

I'm so lonely I'm so lonely I'm so lonely. It's like I'm trapped way way down here in all this brown ooze, and nobody cares.

I don't feel I belong with anyone. I don't feel happy alone. My life seems stupid. I am a joke.

*You're too pretty for your own good.*

I feel things, I still feel things. I can feel you now. I'm here but not here. I'm alive but dead.

My eyes are open and I see that the windshield is streaked with bugs and dirty cleanser. There is a cigarette in the pull-out ashtray of your dash. I hadn't noticed it before. It has some lipstick on the filter.

The sound of cicadas is all around the car. I can smell the pine trees that aren't too far away.

Everything comes up slow and is also speeding by. I can see each pore on your face and the fine hairs across your cheeks. Your mouth is so full and beautiful. At first you don't have any expression, but that starts to change. Finally, your beautiful lips disappear into a straight thin line, an ugly smile.

You are talking to me. You tell me to say things, to do things. I say them and do them. The upholstery on the passenger seat has a crack in it. I am picking out some stuffing. Trying to even it up. The bar below the headrest is pressing against my cheek too hard. I think about that pain. I think about the cut in my mouth, about the taste of blood. I put even more pressure against the bar, try to keep my head steady there. Everything I am goes into what I am doing, away from what you are doing.

After a while, you groan and stop. Bite my shoulder like a puppy. Tell me, "That was great. Do we have any Kleenex?"

From a thousand miles away, I smile. "It's over there," I say, pointing.

We're on the road again in no time. All I can think is how it's funny that when I do something wrong I finally do something right. You are saying, "That was great," over and over again. I make you say it fast, slow, looking at me in different ways. It gives me such a good feeling. I think about the nice things you used to say to me more often.

I think about what I'll do to get that back. But I'm also happy there are still bits of that part of you. It really gives me hope. I can live off things like this for a long time. I'm not greedy.

We don't talk for the rest of the trip, but there's no friction between us like there was before. Square buildings go by. I don't know how anyone finds their way to work every day. Block after block, the place all looks the same.

I run my nails along the hairline around my right ear. When I feel a hair that isn't lining up with the others along the edge, I pull it out. Especially if it feels like it's part of a sideburny kind of thing.

We pass a discount shop I remember buying some knickknacks in for my hope chest. We pick up some drive-thru McDonald's and eat on the road, sharing the large fries. You even tell me I can have the last one.

Finally, we turn off into your mom and dad's subdivision.

You hold my hand up the driveway to the door. We ring the bell. The first thing your mother says is, "What took you so long?" She's looking at me. I can almost hear her sniffing like a dog.

Your dad says, "Now, dear, don't start in already. Let's have a good meal, so they'll want to come back."

He winks at me.

## a place in the sun

I want to be somewhere in your life. I want to do something well. But what more can I do?

Part of my failure is my trying. First of all, I have to prove myself to myself.

Right now I'm such a nobody, stuck in nowhere. But for whatever crazy reason, I have such a strong feeling there's something bigger around the corner. And I know you are a huge part of it. We're destined to be I don't know what.

If I'm nobody now, I'm even less without you.

I just have to find a way to prove myself to you. I'll just have to figure out a way to be exactly what you need to get to the next level. Then I know you'll see that I can be enough.

# TWELVE

**You kiss my mouth deeply.** You kiss my hand. There is nothing else but us. I am wearing a pink-satin négligé from Victoria's Secret. You have no shirt on, but wear tan pants with a pleated front. Your belt and shoes are a rich red-brown.

This is a story for me. This is a story only for me.

You hold me in your arms with a gentle strength. Your movements aren't rushed at all. I close my eyes and you kiss them. I feel butterflies.

We are so in love. Our skin burns just a little as we touch each other. I feel so safe with you. You will take care of me, take care of everything. And together we'll be incredibly strong. I make you more of who you are. You make me complete. We understand this about each other.

So when you touch me, I feel a lightness. I feel so many of my worries float away—I almost want to laugh because I let those things bother me. Now they seem like nothing.

You slowly move a finger along my body, starting from my knee. I lie on my side, so you go along my leg, over my hip, to my waist and up. When you get to my breast, you cup it, feeling the weight in your hand. You bend over and kiss me there. Then your finger continues up, over my neck, caressing my chin and into my mouth.

I suck your finger. But you pull it out after only a few seconds. You don't want to get carried away, and feeling this has always made you a little crazy, made you lose control. You push on my shoulder and have me lie on my stomach. You give me a massage. I drift away.

Then your hands are at my hips. You're lying down beside me and I feel your breath in my hair. One hand slips around and down and you are touching me. I can feel that my négligé is getting wet —sticky and a little cold.

You are licking my shoulders, biting my back, little love bites. Not at all the hard kind that you sometimes do by accident. You are in control, really in control, not needing to feel like you have it, but it's just there.

It feels so good. And I can tell you like making me feel this way. Your body is tight against mine.

You turn me around. We kiss. I touch your nipple, hold your face in my hands. It's so pretty, it almost looks like a girl's. I close my eyes. You slowly take your pants and underwear off. Take my hand and have me touch you.

You pull up the sweet little négligé, and we make love. Really make love. You tell me you love me. You wait for me to come, pause a little and make me come again.

It feels amazing, it just feels so impossibly good. You are my angel. You are my life. You are mine.

*My doll*, you say to me, *was that sweet?* You tell me how tight I am, how delicious, and you come.

We kiss again, stroking each other's backs and nipples, holding each other's hips. The sun bursts in through my bedroom window, setting your skin on fire. Everything sparkles. We fall asleep with you inside, and I dream of never waking up from this, always being here.

# citizen x

You never stop talking about that book on Chikatilo. You keep saying you can't wait till it's winter so you can get me really drunk and do me by some train tracks while I'm passed out.

You keep telling me to try vodka. You say that's how it's done in Russia. You worry that we won't find a place that's cold enough or hidden away enough to really get it right. You're not sure I can down enough to stay out of it.

I like that book, too, but it wasn't *Chikatilo* who had sex with a naked drunk woman in the commie snow. It was a guy the cops *thought* was Chikatilo. Not by name but by what he was doing, dragging a drunk out of a train station like that. The cops secretly watched while he did it to her, hoping to catch their killer in action. He didn't hurt her, though. And when she sobered up, she just walked away from the police station before they'd even asked her anything. Good thinking. Why bother.

Chikatilo had to kill first before he fucked anyone but his wife. And everybody he did was pretty young. Also, he used a knife. And on top of it all, he usually couldn't even get his thing in anyway.

This whole fixation of yours bothers me. I hate when you say you want sex like Chikatilo. You really don't read things very carefully. You get stuff wrong.

# THIRTEEN

**I'm all ready for the date.** I open the door, and here you are, standing with your briefcase. You wear the rattiest clothes I've ever seen you in. Dark and dull. You're a little pale-looking, maybe because of the things you have on. Whatever, you're all jumpy, too.

The briefcase. It's beautiful—very business, very slick. It usually gives you a certain man-on-the-move kind of look. But it's pretty weird, bringing it with you like this for a date, dressed like that.

One time—I don't know if you were setting me up or not—I was snooping around and I found out the briefcase wasn't locked. There was a women's clothing catalogue inside. Its front cover was torn off and the stuff describing the clothes was pasted over with little stories you wrote about the parts of women and girls, and what could be done with those parts. Actually, most of it sounded like my stuff.

In the section of sexy underwear and nighties, young girls' faces were pasted over models' heads. In the section for shirts and pants, breasts and sometimes willies came out between collars and zippers. Same with the dresses. Every once in a while you had written a name underneath.

In the catalogue, two women had penises coming out of their mouths. Some had all their teeth blacked out. Others had their eyes erased. With one, a new background was glued on top, making it so she had no arms. You had blood coming out of the stumps. She was saying, "Eat me."

There was a girl lying down, her knees pulled up, her hands clasped together and tucked under her cheek, almost like a sleeping child, only she was looking straight out, with a sweet sweet little smile. You could still see under the gag drawn over her mouth. Her wrists and ankles were tied like that, too.

It was all so funny. I wanted to know how you'd come up with the idea to do this stuff. It was hilarious and smart. I really wanted you to know that's how I felt. It was like there was finally something we could share. But I also knew you'd kill me for snooping, so I couldn't say anything.

Now here you are at the front door carrying the briefcase, and I'm trying to figure out what it has to do with our date. I'm trying not to smile about it or crack a joke. This is a date, after all, and I don't want to screw it up.

Lately, when we're not meeting up with your friends, when it's the two of us alone, we're barely even together any more. Once we get to a bar, you go in and I wait in the car. If it's a good night, you come out with someone. You'll mess around with her while I sort of hide in the back. I'm supposed to peek over every once in a while to check out what's going on, which is tricky to do because I'm not allowed to be seen by the other girl.

If you ask me what I thought and I tell you, *I didn't see anything, it was too hard*, you get pretty mad. I'm worried that, if my timing's off, and if a girl ever saw me, you'd be even angrier. So far, in the couple of months we've been doing it, I've been lucky.

It's okay, this thing you like to do. Mostly it's just heavy breathing and sticky sounds. For a while, the car jerks around. Maybe the windows steam up. It's pretty boring.

Sometimes she says no, then she stops saying no. A couple of times girls cried after everything. I think they were feeling guilty about cheating on their boyfriends or something.

I don't know why you want me to be there. I try to do what I think you want. I tell you that you were hot with her, that you looked really good. But I don't actually have an opinion. It's as though I'm on drugs, or like I've just woken up from an operation and everything is fuzzy.

I think there are ones I never met, from your nights out with the boys and your prowling around alone. I've seen the clues. I'm not a complete idiot. But I try hard to not let them bug me. None of them mean anything special. Only I can call myself your fiancée. I'm the special one.

I think of all these girls in the same way as the ones in the catalogue. As Jane. Each one is a Jane. She's nobody, she's not special. She is what happens with the police or at a morgue. Somebody nobody knows or really cares about. Something dirty and secret. Jane.

They are bits and pieces pasted here and there. I won't let them get in the way of us. When I saw that catalogue, I felt awesome. It kind of proved that for you this whole thing is like a nutty contest, that's all. For whatever reason, you sometimes want me there in the car with these other girls, but it isn't a big deal.

When we go out to bars to pick them up, we don't call it anything. So when you told me you were taking me out on a date, I took hours to get ready. I made a point of wearing my sexiest things. It took me forever to get my hair right. I really wanted to wow you.

The door is open, with you going from one foot to the other. Nobody else is around. Dad's gone out and Mom is closed up in her room. I try on a smile, but you just say, "Let's go." You are in a real rush, already walking to the driveway.

You barely look at me. What a bummer.

I pick up my things. The raven-blue jacket matches my dress—which is a little low-cut on top and thigh-high down below. My black satin shoes go with the purse. I'm wearing a necklace that used to be my grandmother's. Big deal. You don't even notice.

I spent at least an hour on my hair alone.

"Where are we going?"

"I don't know."

I say, "Ooh, it's a surprise. I like that. It's a surprise even to you. Kind of romantic."

"Yeah," you say.

I don't know why I keep trying. I don't know what I try for. But then you come around to my side of the car and open the door. That really is a nice surprise.

You get into your side. You put the briefcase in the seat behind you. You finally look at me, and say, "You're a little dressed up."

"You said we were going out on a date." Maybe I mixed things up yet again. Maybe this wasn't the night. Maybe you never said, *date*.

"Yeah, that's right. I mean, I didn't mean that kind of date." You look at me again. "We'll have some fun, anyway." You touch my shoulder. It sends shivers through me. Maybe things will be okay.

You kiss me on the cheek and whisper, "You are such a good little girl. You do what the boss man wants."

"And you're the boss. You are the boss." I'm laughing. This could be great. I squeeze your thigh. I feel the muscle under my hand tighten.

You say, "Want some acid?" and of course I say yes, so you give me a tab. Then we're off, in your car.

After a while, I see that the street lights are very close to us. I hear a *whoosh, whoosh, whoosh*, as we pass them. I look up and there are rainbow colours pouring out instead of light, or with the light. And I'm pulled into the colour, into the light.

I'm outside the car, following just behind. I can see through the top, and I'm filled with love. Then I notice that your clothes eat up the light. That you are like a black hole swallowing everything up. You are so dark. And you are getting bigger, getting closer to me.

I must be making scared noises, because you are singing to me from inside the car. It's a lullaby. You look over to me with a sweet little smile and I realize I'm back in the car, back beside you. Safe again.

There is light coming out of your face.

I can see only your head and hands—your clothes are gone, and with them your body.

"Let's be astronauts going off for an adventure," you say. "You're the first girl in space. You've been chosen because you're so helpful. I'm lucky to have you as my partner on the voyage." You say all this in an official kind of voice. I feel your hand on mine, then it's back on the wheel.

I close my eyes. This is too good. My lungs take in air that is sweet. The shattered haloes of light are thrown over me *whoosh, whoosh, whoosh*, and each time I am reborn. Each time I am more beautiful and pure.

I knew we would come back together the way we were. I have to admit I was starting to lose hope, I thought maybe I'd screwed up so bad and you wouldn't put up with any more. What a surprise. What a perfect, perfect night.

I imagine the catalogue Janes locked up behind us as the real girls, all of them green with envy, crowded in the back seat. Trapped in that briefcase. They've had a taste of you, and know how good I have it.

I feel the car turning right and I hear a buzzing and I know we are on Powerline Road. Without opening my eyes I see the hydro pylons marching beside us with their ugly, endless wires. The snap and buzz of them take over the crickets.

"Where are we going, again?"

"On an adventure. Where no girl has gone before." You laugh a little. It sounds like a cherub's laugh. I have cherub wallpaper at home, and I see them all now, giggling like Pillsbury Doughboys.

Does it mean we can forget the stuff that's happened between us? Are we starting totally from scratch? We are launching off into space—the only man and woman—to start all over again on another planet. We'll play cards and truth-or-dare out there in the universe until we land. Every once in a while, we might have to freeze ourselves so we can stay young. Once we find a planet we can settle down on, we can think of having kids.

And we can forget about the other girls, and you'll forgive me for all I've done that's pushed you from me. It isn't that you've done anything wrong, it has always really been me. I left you with no choices. I know that, but I'm forgetting that, too.

I can feel all this old stuff pulling away from my brain. I can see it, brown and sludgy, coming out of my nose and floating out the window. The power lines burn it. A smell like a million flowers fills the air.

My head gets lighter. I start to laugh. Whoosh and buzz and chirrup mix together and become the music on the radio. I move to the sound of my beginning again. The light pours on me.

"Yes, little girl, it's going to be an adventure. Let's go out there and make our dreams come true. Let's show the bastards what we can do. Fuck them!"

Your hand is under my dress. I'm nowhere and everywhere. I could swallow the world.

I start to sing one of my dad's favourite songs, "A Kiss to Build a Dream On." I used to dance to it when I was little, and he would laugh. I would hug myself, sway around and blow my cheeks up big like Louis Armstrong.

When I'm finished, you say, "What a pretty voice. And pretty girl."

"That song's for you," I say. "That song is what I felt from the first time we were together. You're everything." I look inside you by looking at your eyes. It's like I've gotten right into you.

You look away.

You snort and say, "Sometimes I wonder about you."

We both laugh. I feel like I would shatter if I was any happier.

We are driving and driving. There are no limits to where we can go.

You say, "There's something I want to show you. I found it for you."

"Okee doke," I say.

A house. A view. A ring. Your love.

You pull to the side of the road and tell me we're getting out. I

follow you to the back of the car. You open the trunk. There is a girl
inside. I don't know if she's knocked out or dead.

"Let's get another one." You sound so light, so easy about it.

"Okay."

I am trembling, which you don't notice.

I run back to the passenger's side.

# dear

Any advice about a man is all about how to get him and how to keep him. There isn't really any word about what you do with him once he's yours. I read the columns. I try to figure it out. But it's a real guessing game, even for experts.

I do what I can. Sometimes I wonder what I'm getting out of the deal. But I'd be nothing alone. And chances are, with my luck, I'd be stuck always being alone, even when I decided I wanted to be with a guy.

You have your good points, I can't forget that. It's just . . . I'm sad. I'm crushed. I've put so much of myself into you. You're everything I have. I'm feeling pretty blue. It seemed like things were going better than I could have dreamed, and then *wham*.

I have to say that this whole experience makes me see things in a different way. It makes me wish I could be alone, surrounded by animals. It's not that I like them better than people. It's just that they disappoint me less.

The one thing is you really have to depend on me all of a sudden.

Since that night, you go out of your way to be nice. It's just too bad it took something like this for you to show you care for me. You give me some respect, now.

Maybe, just maybe, with this terrible thing behind us, you'll see how it is when you're sweet to me, and we can stay this way. Maybe after a while we can forget the bad stuff. I know you've always wanted to be the rebel, but now we know it should only go so far. It's like we took a dare, and we dared too much.

I'm telling you, they never talk about stuff like this in phys ed.

# FOURTEEN

We are children, you, me, Adrian. The same age,
small, like birds.

Three of us in a spring field . . .

In a sunny old attic somewhere . . .

Wherever we are, our hair explodes with light—we are angels.

The grass is fresh, silk against our skin . . .

The floor is covered in layers of downy dust . . .

Whatever place we lie in, it holds us gently. We are pure, and the
world is here for us. None of us wears clothes, and we don't even
care.

. . . I know where, we're on a river bank. We go swimming. We run
our tongues over each other's nipples, wanting to see them rise.
Wanting to feel the buttons harden. Each one wanting to feel the tin-
gling deep inside when it's our turn to be licked.

We paint each other with mud.

Adrian needs to pee. You and I watch, curious. Later, you need to
pee and the two girls watch. You do tricks, and we all laugh. Your
spray comes out in bursts, just like your laugh.

It's as though there's nobody else left in the world, and that's perfect. The day will never end.

We eat a picnic, two flat-chested girls and a beautiful boy. Adrian
and I have mud caked in our hair, which is piled on top of our heads,

out of the way. You have lines and dots smeared all over your body, proof you are a warrior.

Cheez Whiz on Wonderbread. Kool-Aid. Oreo cookies. A meal for royal children free to demand and receive. We leave crumbs and cups behind, running straight into the river. Adrian and I wash out our hair and scrub your skin. Everything feels good and new again. After some fooling around, we throw our little bodies on the bank to be dried by the sun.

Adrian wakes up first. I see her mouth, then realize a sound is coming from it. Her eyes are open, round, and she is really pale. The sound she is making is quiet, like the noise I imagine comes from a dog whistle.

You still sleep.

I look where Adrian is looking. There is a man I do not know. He's doing something I've never seen before, but it makes me scared. Like her, I am frozen. Unlike her, I don't scream. I am wishing to disappear.

He is looking at all of us, one at a time. Not even you are safe. His pants are down around his knees. He has long white hair and a neat beard and his penis in his hands. Adrian and I only know your sweet penis. It doesn't seem possible that it's the same thing as we're seeing now. We can't believe the size. Or the colour.

He is rocking slightly back and forth. His hand races up and down, like a cartoon character's. There are noises coming from deep in his throat.

If it weren't for what he was doing, I would almost think he was god, or Santa. I want to cry.

He is looking right at you when you finally wake up. He laughs and pulls his pants up, but he doesn't fasten them. He walks over to us.

You are very angry, and you pick up the stick that had been your sword before.

"Get outta here," you yell. "Get out."

He looks surprised, and has a smile on his face. "Hey, I won't hurt you," he says.

You say, "I know you. You're the perv."

Adrian reaches over and takes my hand.

The next time you tell him to get out, your voice is choked up. Your eyes look the same as a doll's and your cheeks are very red. You jab the stick into the ground and show your teeth. You are shaking.

Adrian and I stroke each other's hair and cry softly.

He looks at us and seems very happy. "What's going on over here, girls?"

You look, too, and he grabs at your stick. The first time, he misses. On the second try he's got a hold of it. You do your best to keep it, but you've lost before you started. It was no real tug of war. He is the grown-up.

When he walks over to Adrian and me, he brings you along in front of him, pinning your arms behind your back. He still looks very pleased with us. He says you're like a wiggly worm, you're a real boy, you're his little tiger.

He says you remind him of when he was young.

"Watch it, chief," he says.

I want to close my eyes until this time passes. I want to see everything. I make a deal with myself. My eyes are wide, but part of me is somewhere else. I can hear the two girls whisper to each other.

He is right up to us now. He orders you to take his shoes off, then his pants and underwear. The shoes go side by side. Each sock is to be balled up and put in its matching shoe. Then the pants, nicely folded, go on top of the shoes. Then the underwear is to be put on top of the pants.

It takes you a couple of tries to get it exactly right. The man says, "I guess boys aren't used to folding laundry."

He tells you to kiss him there, "And don't bite, now. Don't think I don't know what you're thinking. It would mean big trouble, you understand?"

You only kiss him a couple of times, dry little pecks with a nasty look on your face. He doesn't mind. He picks you up and throws you in the water. He might be old, but he is very strong. You come out and run to us. He picks you up again. The tossing goes on until you come close to us and collapse, water-drenched, spitting and exhausted.

That's when he bends down and starts pawing the two girls at the same time, one hand each. His palms are rough, and he pushes down hard. Our muscles tighten, so he says, *Relax now.*

Like a spell, *Relax now, relax.* It's hard to believe that the hard touch and gentle voice come from the same person.

We are tired from crying, tired from fear. We let him do what he wants. It all seems far away to me. He shoves some fingers up inside. He does the same to Adrian.

He makes us go on our bellies. He pinches our bums, squeezes them, pulls the cheeks apart. He sticks his fingers into that end. He goes over and does it to you, too. The two girls are afraid to move, even though we know this is the best chance we have to escape.

"Bastard," you say. "Dirty perv." Your face turns as far around as it can go and you try to spit at him, but the stuff just goes down your chin.

Now he is on top of Adrian, rubbing himself back and forth. "You're nice," he says to her. "You're the nicest. Is that your mommy's hair you've got?"

He pulls my hand from Adrian's, gouging my fingers from between hers, one by one. I try hard to keep a hold, but I can't, I can't.

He sits on her back and holds her arms. He is rubbing himself over her back, in her hair. He pokes his penis against her bum.

It sounds like she can't breathe right. "Calm down, now," he says. "Everything's okay. This is nice. This'll be nice." He looks over and winks at me. "You don't mind if she and I go play by ourselves awhile."

He reaches over and slaps me, hard. I've never felt something so strongly before. I am inside my body again.

While he holds Adrian's hands with one of his, he picks up the stick. Anchoring the other end in the ground, he snaps it in the middle, using a quick kick with his foot.

He takes the first piece and puts it into your bum, then puts the other piece into mine. He makes Adrian frog march away, disappearing into the bush.

You don't look at me. I can tell you are crying anyway. I'm not, any more. I put my arm around your shoulders. You put yours around my waist. Neither of us says anything. We know Adrian will never come back, and we're swallowed in a grief much older than us.

But I'm also thinking, *Why not me?*

Why am I never good enough?

## the sadness inside us all

They are all in a panic about Adrian. She isn't the kind of girl to just run away. We've gone on a couple of the searches. I've put up posters and spoken at two school assemblies in the smelly old gym with wooden bleachers that really need some paint.

I miss her.

The school is giving lessons in street-proofing again—always after the fact, when it's too late. What they should teach is love-proofing. That wouldn't have worked for her.

It was destiny.

You cry over Adrian, too. You talk about the perfect moments we all shared. I know you're including that night, which bothers me a little, but we all have our own ways to grieve. They told us that at school, saying they hope for the best, but they know what students are thinking about, and that we can't help but to think of the worst, sometimes. The positive and the negative have to make room for each other, they said, and that's okay.

# F I F T E E N

*Normal rules are for normal people.* I don't know why you have to keep hearing it. I'm getting tired of saying those words. You hold me tight. Your lips quiver. You repeat it to me, as if it wasn't something you told me ages ago. As if it's something new.

What we did was wrong. We both feel bad. But we did it and now it's too late—there's nothing we can change. We have to move on. Why bother making excuses for the past. We were other people for a few crazy minutes . . . we were on drugs . . . things just weirded out. We lost control. It's that simple. We won't do it ever again.

Of course I'll always be sad. At the same time, I'm surprised at how little I actually feel nowadays. At how numb I am to most things. It's a deep, sleepy feeling. In school, I catch myself in the middle of talking to someone. I snap out of some kind of spell, blathering away. It's scary, but of course I'm not saying anything important anyway. You know. *It's so sad. I'm really worried. Where could she be?* Over and over again. Auto-pilot.

It's very hard to concentrate.

Meanwhile, you're picking at your cuticles till they bleed, sometimes in front of everybody. You start another cigarette before you've finished the last one. You're so forgetful now, and leave things around that you shouldn't. I'm your maid, cleaning up after you, making sure we're safe. I'm the mother you never had.

I worry that all your panicky behaviour will make people notice us. You've got to calm down. It tires me out even more, trying to make you feel better, trying to get you to focus. It bugs me. I need you to be on top of things. To think straight.

Luckily, everyone around us is so incredibly thick. I can't believe they haven't figured out what's happened. I guess it's a good thing we're living in a world of zombies.

We go through the examples we know of other people who have been through stuff like this. We talk about what they did, where they aced it and where they messed up. We clip news articles and look for clues. The most important thing is to keep cool, to act normal, whatever that's supposed to be.

Normal can be pretty unpredictable.

Police say they first wondered about a guy because he was at a dead kid's funeral. Another guy is found guilty because people thought it was weird he didn't go to the funeral.

I read about a teenager who was kidnapped and made into a sex slave for seven years. Finally, she escaped. The case went to court. The one lawyer didn't like how she was on the stand—she had totally no emotions. This lawyer was worried that her victim didn't act like people thought a former sex slave should. Like there are rules in a book about it. I laughed hard at that one, I'll tell you.

Dear boyfriend, we are freaks. And if we can pull this off, we're even bigger freaks. There have been many freaks before us, and many will follow. We are not alone. And some people are famous because being a freak means you're more interesting than the walking dead are. The ones who are so proud of being normal.

Freaks rule. Please just calm down.

I rub your back. I whisper in your ear. We haven't had sex in a while. You need me too much right now, but you need me, and that's nice, even if it does mean you can't be my sexy big man. I promise I'll help get that part of you back.

I brush away your tears. I kiss them from your eyes.

I say, "I know. Sh, sh, sh. I know."

And you need me.

If only *this* part could always be normal for us. Your hand runs softly down my arm. You gather up my hair and smell it. You call me an angel. You tell me I'm so good to you.

Tonight we're going to take a long walk, hand in hand. We'll go to the place where we got her, and we'll talk. I think this time we'll fool around. We'll make love there, in her memory. I think you can do it if I explain it that way. And if I'm lucky, you'll say my name, not hers. You'll look at me and see no one else, no ghost, no vision.

I'm not sure what I should wear. I want to look sexy, but not too much, not slutty. We're still in mourning.

I'm brushing my hair out. I've got some eyeliner on and some water-proof mascara. I won't curl my eyelashes. There's a hint of blush, and I've put on foundation just to even things out. I'll go with clear lip shimmer.

I'm wearing my mother's baby pearls and a navy suit. Low pumps.

I don't know if you're fussing about what you'll wear, the way you used to for me a long time ago. I'm hoping so, even though I don't expect it.

We've gone on such crazy jags. I guess we're just two doomed, tragic lovers. I'd love to go somewhere for advice, but there's nowhere to go. I'll have to do the best with what I know.

This is the time to really prove myself. Even with everything, I'm starting to feel like maybe I can do it. Have to start making supper. Pork chops, scalloped potatoes, applesauce, corn and fresh green beans. Your favourites.

# education

Days go by. Things keep going. The excitement about Adrian dies down. Posters of her are still up, and the newspapers still write about her. But in school we've got to get ready for final exams, and we're concentrating on that now.

The girls and I talk about her. Try to figure out where she could be. Some of their ideas are really stupid. Because I was her best friend, everyone wants to talk to me. But I still know them for the stuck-up bitches they really are. I think they go back to their dull safe houses and get wet thinking about all the nasty things that might have happened to Adrian. Imagining it happening to them.

I hope that all this won't hurt my grades too much. I've been handing essays in late, and not doing as well as I could on tests. I'm a bit worried about what's going to happen to my average. The principal told me they'll adjust things because of my situation. He's pretty nice. He knows what Adrian means to me.

And what about when I finish school? I want to marry you, settle down. But I can't get over the feeling there's something more, something big. I keep seeing myself on TV, showing people things. Teaching them, somehow.

# S I X T E E N

**We are in a room together, hands cuffed behind our backs.** We sit at a table with a bare bulb hanging down over it. There is a wall behind you with a one-way mirror running from one end to the other. There are nothing but greys in here, and the lousy smell of old cigarettes.

We sit for hours. No one comes in or out. We don't speak to one another, partly because we don't want to be bothered, but also because we know there might be someone watching us, listening for what we say. We are together in this room, both pretending to be alone. Actually, being stuck with each other makes each of us feel more lonely than if we were by ourselves. Being with someone you hate who you used to love does that.

It's almost a relief, really, being here. I feel sleepy but serene.

I'm all fuzzy. I don't remember any explanation about what we're doing here. I don't remember an arrest. This forgetfulness isn't so surprising. It's been hard to keep track over the last few weeks. Everything's been swirling together and swallowed up. These days, I take some pills and drink quite a bit, too, just to get by.

I haven't been to the bathroom in here, and I don't need to, so it hasn't been that long. My wrists itch and I'm worried my nose is runny, but that's about it. I keep sniffing hard. I know me doing this must drive you crazy. You're really hyper about women being all lady-like, at least in public. Knowing this makes me do it harder than I have to.

You are so selfish. I can't believe that I used to think you were strong. You are a slobbery mess right now. You are like a snarly old dog trying to scare somebody away, but it's a joke. You have no teeth, and everyone can see the gunk in your eyes.

Idiot.

It's like you put me under a spell, and now the spell is broken.

You make me sick. Woof woof, poodle boy.

You betrayed me. You betrayed me.

Meanwhile, I've lost the one person who understood me at all, even if it was only a little. The one person I've ever really loved, I know that now. You loved her, too, in your sorry-assed way. But nothing you had could compare to the love Adrian and I shared. That's because she loved me back.

Now I understand everything she tried to tell me about you.

Finally, the door opens.

Three guys walk in. One stands behind you. The others take a couple of chairs and sit down. They look at us for a long time. You keep your head down.

I watch the men. My nerves only show behind my back, where I'm pinching my hands, digging my nails into my wrists. I can imagine the crescent shapes I make in the skin. I try to think of the pattern. I try to press down in different ways and think about how it might look. I think very hard, to keep my mind off things.

The guy standing up says, "We know about the bodies." He's looking at the cop closest to me.

You snap out of it. You sneer. Your head tilts. You look at them sideways. "These handcuffs hurt."

He kicks at the back of your chair. I know you're clamping your hands together so they won't shake. I know you're biting the inside of your mouth. You do additions and subtractions in your head.

The three men are having fun with us. They are sitting back, waiting us out. But neither of us gives.

The guy behind you says, "You have the bodies. We've heard about them. You've got to prove it's true."

They're asking us for evidence. It all must be a bluff. At this moment, we depend on each other. Right now, when I'd do almost anything to get away from you, the one thing I won't do is confess. I'd be in trouble. But I don't think I should be blamed. I've got too much to live for.

Plus, I'm the girl.

"We're taking the cuffs off, but you're not going anywhere," he says.

You shake your head a bit. "Listen, what have you heard?" you ask.

The standing one punches you on the arm. He says, "Stud," and winks at you. He crouches down and unlocks the cuffs. Then he comes around and does the same for me.

They get out of the room. The light bulb is switched off, and some fan-shaped wall sconces set on dim come on. They pipe in soft music, not really our type, something you'd hear late at night on an E-Z rock station. What some boring yuppie paper-pusher would think of as romantic.

We rub our wrists for a while, looking at each other from the corners of our eyes.

The thought of you touching me is repulsive. I feel clammy.

"What should we do?" Your hands are now in your pockets, and you're looking down at the floor.

I come to you and kiss you hard on the mouth.

"Let's get through this," I say.

"Whatever."

I've gone through with things you wanted that I didn't really want lots of times. There's something kind of nice about you having to go through with something, too. Not out of love this time, but for both of us it's for ourselves. Which I guess is a kind of love in the end. It's like we're finally even. Equal.

Actually, you have a hard time keeping it up. You say, "What's gotten into you?" You say, "I'm not used to doing it with girls like this."

I'm not waiting for your orders any more. "Sh, sh," I say. "C'mon, you can do it. Come on, doesn't that feel nice?"

I lick you all over. I lose track of things a little, and hear you yelp and realize I've bitten you, hard.

So that's how it feels, to hurt someone that way. Now I get what you like. You make more sense. Maybe I can work through all this negativity and see something else to love in you. Maybe our relationship can be new again. Things can change.

I don't want to be a failure. I've put so much already into you and me, I shouldn't throw that away. We know so much about each other. And I don't want to give people a reason to laugh right in my face. I don't want them to say I was dumped. That I'm used goods. I don't want to be stuck with my parents, alone.

Things just might work out after all.

When someone loves someone, even though sometimes it can turn to a sort of hate, a lot of the time they want it to stay together. It's like an investment.

## getting caught

What would it take?

I go through what could happen almost every night.

I dream about it.

I jump when the doorbell rings.

My heart sinks when you come in, but at least it slows down, too.

You barely speak to Mom and Dad now.

You walk in, say hi, and come straight up to my room, where you know I'll be. We hold each other tight. You tell me how much I mean to you.

My parents say they know what we must be going through. How different things will be from now on. "My baby, I'm so sorry," they say to me, with tears in their eyes. Liars.

My mind wanders. I feel eyes at the window the same as I used to when I was a kid.

# SEVENTEEN

They've got one. The paper says:

> A young woman's nude body was found in Bruker Creek
> late last night. There were signs of violence.
>
> The gruesome discovery was made by 3 teenagers going
> to a field party at roughly 2 a.m. Police are releasing few de-
> tails at this time. A statement to the media indicates they
> have some leads regarding the victim's identity, but nothing
> has been confirmed.
>
> A local teen, Adrian Phillips, 17, disappeared May 20.
> While several search parties have been organized in the past
> 3 weeks, the popular Geneva Heights high-school student is
> still missing.
>
> Police have ruled out the possibility the teen ran away.
> "She's a good girl," said Sergeant Ron Gelder, who is lead-
> ing the investigation into Adrian's disappearance. "There's
> no indication she would be the type to leave so suddenly.
> The family is close. She was working hard to finish school."
>
> Her family told this paper that they still have great hopes
> Adrian is alive. "She's a fighter," her father, Nick Phillips,
> said. "She'll be back."

Right now you are at work in the city. I'm not sure if papers there
will run the story. I don't know whether to call. I decide not to.

I tell Mom I have really bad menstrual cramps, and she lets me stay
home.

117

Things are seriously fucked.

I am curled up on my bed. I'm looking at my shelves of gifts from you, and I'm holding one of the bears. For some reason I can't cry. I'm fidgeting. With my hair. With my arms. I have to watch that I don't pull too hard or cut too deep.

On my arms I draw tiny lines beside each other. If someone didn't look very close, it would look like a rash. I go over the same twenty or so marks so that I won't make too many. This time, I'm using a steak knife.

I check out my hair. I was trying to get the hairline to even out, but now I think that the place where the part starts looks too square, and I'm trying to round it out. It's tricky, and I really have to pay attention, which is good.

The teddy bear is on my lap. It's the white one. The first one you gave me. I named him Buddy, telling you he'd keep me company when you weren't able to visit me. I remember laughing, telling you how much I loved Buddy but that no matter how hard he tried he could never kiss as good as you.

I need you so much. We need each other, depend on each other. It's when things get really rough that a person realizes what's important. It's in bad times that people come together. We've definitely had our ups and downs, but I really need to not forget the ups, even with all that's happened.

I've had to mature all of a sudden, and I can finally see what love truly means, how it's not just about feeling good all of the time. I've been such a baby, such a little girl.

The day crawls along. No one comes by to ask questions. Mom leaves me alone. I can't think of anyone to call. I wish I could talk to Adrian.

Why does life have to be so complicated?

What are we supposed to do?

Things were complicated even before all this happened. Now it's just totally mind-boggling.

A body was found in the creek. Not much of a surprise, I guess. But I've lived here my whole life, and I know just about everywhere there is to go party. I don't know anything about any clearing along the creek. Did they make that up? Why would they lie? Bodies float. Who knows where they get to over a few weeks?

Blah blah blah blah blah.

I'm making myself crazy.

My hairline is now officially uneven. I better knock off the plucking.

I put on my walkman and my favourite CD. Closing my eyes I see you with Adrian, and the other one.

You pull to the side of the road and tell me we should get out. I follow you to the back of the car. You open the trunk. There is this girl inside. She is wearing tarty make-up and slutty clothes. She looks like a twelve-year-old passing for thirty. I can't tell if she's out of it or dead.

"Let's get another one." You sound so easy about it.

"Okay."

I start shaking, but you don't notice. I think I know right then it'll be Adrian.

I'm still tripping on acid. Right up until when you opened the trunk, I was thinking we might get back to the way things were in the old days.

What a mean trick.

Adrian is at the ice-cream store. She'll be walking out the back door with the garbage when she closes up, so we park the car there about ten minutes before she finishes. You tell me to give you a blow job, which of course I do.

I try to think of Adrian as a Jane. I'm trying to get ready, to be prepared.

We call her over when she leaves the store. We open the doors and get out. The three of us talk about something, I don't know what, I can't remember. Then she gets into the back and I click the seat into position and sit in the passenger seat and you are starting the car and we all go off somewhere.

Everything happens very fast. And she's so cool with it. That makes me feel easier about things—I start to believe she must know what's going on. The two of you set this whole thing up. I regret working things out with her. This could be it for me—you're getting the one you really want. I start to get mad.

This is exactly what I'm trying not to think about. I shut off the music and get up from bed. I should go downstairs and see if I can eat.

Walking through the living room, I decide to turn on the TV. I watch the news at noon. They still won't say a name. They give a description: brown hair, five-two, eighteen to twenty-four, Asian.

It wasn't her they found, it was the other one. I'm really surprised she was that old. No sign yet of Adrian and her glorious red hair.

I guess we're still fucked, but we're not as fucked.

I go back upstairs and fall asleep, forgetting to eat.

# grief

What kind of sadness have you brought on my parents' house? How can my mother and father keep stumbling around, innocent children who don't know about our evil?

Mom says, "Honey, why are you so blue? You've got to think of your school. Adrian would want that."

My father hugs me around the shoulders. He presses his face into my hair. He tells me he's there for me. I try to pull away.

Time is sludge sticking to my skin. I am sinking. I am sinking into it, praying to be swallowed up. Hoping for some sweet release.

"Sweetie, we can get you some help," they say.

I want to laugh in their faces, my baby mom's and baby dad's. I want to spit on their graves, but even though they're dead, they're not buried yet.

I live in a house of zombies, stuck with a blood-sucking zombie boyfriend. I wish I could take Adrian's place. She's such a lucky girl.

# EIGHTEEN

**I might as well have your hands around my throat.** You might as well be some evil stranger, plotting to hurt me.

I think an evil stranger would be easier to take than this. It serves me right, what happened. I'm such an idiot. I've been so slow. It wasn't like I didn't know there were problems all along. I just didn't want to see.

And even now that I've figured stuff out, I still love you. I still see the guy you were. I'm hopeless.

I dream, I dream of escape. It would break my heart to never see you again, but at least I could breathe. I've had it with this waiting. I've had it with school, with living at home, with all these problems and with you. I'd have to go somewhere no one would expect, where no one would come looking. I could go back to school there under another name, upgrade my average. I could go to college. Meet a guy. For all anyone would know, I could say I was meeting up with Adrian. You would know it wasn't true, but what could you do about it? Tell people I'm lying?

It might work like this—I wait till Mom and Dad go on another trip. I cut my hair, colour it, put in my brown-tinted contacts that only you know about. I wear some of Mom's clothes. I get on a bus to as far away as possible. I phone home and leave messages about how I'm going to a party, how I met so-and-so downtown, how the weather has been. They won't figure anything out until it's way too late, when they're back home. Finally, I'll call and tell them I've met up with Adrian, that I'm not coming back. That Adrian and I had planned it like this all along.

Every once in a while, Adrian and I send postcards from different places around the world. It would give some comfort to her parents, who have always been good to me.

I'd like to do that.

My new boyfriend wouldn't be as good-looking as you, or as sexy as when you and I started out. But I could go for a calm, boring kind of guy in my life right now. I could go for someone who won't make me lose sleep every night. Someone who isn't about to snap.

You could go on with your life, too. All those times you told me I dragged you down. You'd be free. You could do all those great big-man things you always say you're about to do. Drive over to my parents' and get some sympathy. Go be another Chikatilo for all I care, diddling dead little kids.

I will never truly fall in love again. Life as it was will never be again. Before I escape, I touch my stuffed animals. I trace my finger over the dainty locks on my old diaries. I look at my figurines and know something is lost forever. I'll never be a little girl again.

You've killed something in me, but something else has taken over. I close my eyes and see things I could never make up. I guess you have more imagination than I ever gave you credit for.

I would have given you everything, but what I had to give, you didn't want. You only want what you can take. You want to break people and throw them away. You're an empty little shit.

Wait, wait, I don't mean any of that. I love you. I've been drinking down in the basement rec room. You'll be over soon. I've got to straighten up. Pull myself together.

Let me pretend. Let me walk out the door. Walk down the street. Everything slow-motion, the seconds dragging out to hours. My hair cool on my neck. I wear high heels and they click on the pavement.

Remember the scene in that movie, *Tokyo Decadence*, where the little Japanese girl is walking up the hills? She has those funny small jerky steps because of her sweet pastel-yellow shoes with the big bows. She's also kind of whacked out on stuff she took to calm down. But she looks so cute, so innocent. That's how I want to look.

I am walking out the door in slow sweet little up-and-down steps. And I just keep walking and walking up and down the hills until I get to a whole other world I can lose myself in. People won't know me and I can start over. They'll find what's good in me and won't remind me of all my faults.

If I'm lucky, I'll meet someone like my angel, Adrian. Maybe she'll be reincarnated or something. She'll hug me and tell me everything's okay, she understands. We'll go shopping together and have a gas.

You've got to let me get these things out. You've got to let me think them. Anyway, it's not like you can read my mind. You don't know me at all. You used to tell me you did, and I believed you for a long time, but now we both know it's not true.

I'm running into the arms of some man who understands me. He takes me to his house and puts me in the guest room. It's mostly decorated like Ikea, and it's very cozy. He's a real gentleman. I stay in that house for a long time. Then one night by the fire he bends over and gives me a gentlemanly kiss. He falls in love with me. I take care of his house. I do some crafts. I visit with neighbours when I want. He is never jealous, because he knows how much I love him. I have lots of friends. We have a couple of kids, and they adore me.

And, you know, this might sound crazy, but it still could be you. When I imagine my dream life, I can't help seeing your face sometimes.

We all make mistakes. Let's just start new. Maybe we both could change our names or something. Get away completely from our parents and everybody. I'll be your one special girl, the one who keeps you, and you'll be my only man.

We would really take care of each other, because there could be big trouble if we got each other mad. You'd treat me well, because you couldn't afford not to.

I feel so strong with you now in a way, and that's not something just to chuck out.

## split personality

You are the best thing that ever happened to me. You are the worst. I've never felt more alive than when I'm with you. Nobody could make me feel more dead.

I'm scared sometimes you want me dead.

You are so tender with me now, it scares me more than just about anything else could. I'm afraid of what you might be working up to.

But I'm addicted.

You talk about Adrian all of the time. It's not the same as when she was alive, which in some ways makes it worse. I thought at least what happened would make things final. But how am I supposed to compete with a ghost, an angel, a spirit who visits your dreams?

It makes me want to give up. It makes me want to do something that will end things one way or the other. But then you call me up, crying, telling me how much I mean to you. "The best of times, the worst of times," for sure.

# NINETEEN

**Until last year, I didn't swim with goggles.** It's amazing what I see when I wear them. Everything's so clear, but colours are kind of weird, with a bluishness all over, like a coating of hair gel. I see people jump in, covered in tiny air bubbles, their bathing suits sometimes flattened against them, sometimes ballooning out. Arms and legs move in ways not seen on land. And even if it seems kind of strange to say so, sounds come out better, too, with goggles on.

I swim underwater for a long time almost every day now. I like seeing the world from down there. I turn around and look at the surface and wonder about dolphins, fish and whales. I wonder what it would be like to never have to come up for air. To always feel water pressing against my skin. To see what they see.

I see myself floating around, then happily sinking to the bottom of the pool. My arms would be stretched out. My legs together. My hair like a pale fire around my head. I would want my eyes open, because I'd want to see everything there was to see on this side of life and the other.

I dream sometimes about swimming underwater. Lately, I spend most of my time walking around feeling like I am underwater. Like there's a bubble between me and everything else. I can go around and not hear sound for days.

School is over and there hasn't been anything more about the brown-haired girl. They still don't even know who she was, or where she's from. I guess you picked a good one. Have to give you credit there.

I did okay on my exams, but I'm taking a couple of summer-school courses to improve my overall grades. I'm taking a year off before college or whatever. Mom and Dad are okay with my decision. They say I had a big year with all that happened. And also this way it'll be easier to plan for the wedding.

Weeks have passed, and after a few questions, life goes on. Mom and Dad worry about my being down. They tell me maybe I need to see someone even before we go to marriage counselling. They tell me this is no frame of mind to get married in, that I should do my very best to snap out of it. That it isn't fair to you.

But who will be my maid of honour, now that there's no Adrian? I'm thinking maybe no one. That would be the best thing. Everyone would understand. It's hard to get excited about the "special day," though. It's hard to get excited about anything any more. We have to go through with it, though. We've got to show everyone that things are okay. That we're getting on with life. Anyway, too much could happen if we broke up. It would be way too scary, thinking all the time that you could spill the beans any minute, and I wouldn't be there to stop you.

You haven't even given me a ring yet, and now I don't even bother asking about it. We're stuck with each other.

We go drinking with friends. We dance. We party every chance we get. Whatever we do, that night comes leaking through the cracks.

You ask me to be our Adrian, or the brown-haired girl, or some-body else. You tell me to tell you I like what you do. I tell you they like it. Then I watch you put me through what it is they're sup-posed to like, your Janes. You have me feel what they supposedly like. It makes my skin crawl. So, you know, I take off. I kind of go swimming.

Adrian is in the back seat. It's been a while since we picked her up. Even as the time passes right in front of my face, I lose track of exactly what happens. She's got me singing some song from when we were kids.

Suddenly there's a thump, and she asks what it is. You say nothing. The road is smooth, and we didn't run over anything. Then there's another thump, followed by a moan.

"Jesus Christ, what is that?" Adrian asks.

And it all starts crashing. My mind had silk curtains wrapped around it, making this evening soft and sexy. Up to now, whatever you threw at me, I made the best of it. In this moment, it's all torn away and left in tatters. There is no more pretending. There is nothing left to make the best of.

And I am saying, "Shut up. Shut the fuck up, bitch."

And you are saying, "Keep cool. Hey, you two, keep your shirts on."

You look at the road. You say, "I'm playing a joke on a buddy."

Somehow, Adrian believes you. She's always made a point of telling me how she doesn't find your jokes funny. Or maybe in this case it's that she's willing to give you anything. "Well, I think the joke's over," she says.

I can tell you're trying to figure out what to do.

I say under my breath, so quiet a human can't hear, "Shut the fuck up. Shut the fuck up. Shut the fuck up." It calms me down on the outside. On the inside, I am starting to slip away, going to a quieter place away from this car. I'm above the roof again, able to see in.

I see that I've got my fingernails digging hard into my forearms, which are crossed over like maybe they would be if I were in the middle of some weird ritual. It takes away a bit of the tension, so I let myself do it.

We drive along. There are a few more thumps out of the trunk.

Adrian is pretty pissed off. She says, "Guys, the joke is over. Cut it out. Stop, now."

Is it my job to talk to her? I can't. I have to concentrate on what

I'm saying in my head. I can only think of these little marks I'm making on my arms.

You try some chit-chat, but it's not really working. I look down from where I am floating and see Adrian bending forward. Her hair shoots out at me. It's coming up to strangle me. I grab it and pull it hard but now I'm in the front seat and I've pulled her head so it's between you and I. There's a knife in my hand.

"Shit," you say. "What the fuck are you doing?"

I see that you are talking to Adrian. You are mad at Adrian. I have done something right.

The car swerves when Adrian tries to fight. Then I dig the knife a little into her throat, and she stays still.

She is looking at me with great big eyes. All she can say is, "Why? Why? Why?" Then she is quiet. She's doing everything she can not to cry.

"I don't know," I say. "Why anything?"

I say, "Do you feel like a rat?"

She looks at me for a while. She's confused. She's trying to figure it out. She says no.

"Forget it," I say.

She looks so sad and now I feel very sorry for her. I start to cry, but I keep the knife in place.

"Don't," you say, and I stop crying.

You seem to know where we're going, and finally we get there.

You turn to Adrian and say, "Look, sorry, she's really freaked out these days," pointing to me. "She's on acid. She doesn't mean it.

"Let's get out and party a little," you say, then look at me. "Stop being silly and put the knife down."

We are in the woods, far from any home. We get out of the car. You pull a big bottle from under your seat.

I mumble, "Sorry, Adrian, I'm so sorry." I'm not sure she can hear.

You try to get Adrian to drink as much as possible. But it seems as though I keep getting the bottle, and I down as much as I can. You are getting mad at me.

Adrian is obviously thrown by what I did in the car. She sits where she can always keep her eye on me, and at the same time keep her distance. After she's a bit drunk, she remembers the thump that got us into trouble in the first place. She asks about it.

"Oh, shit," you say, "thanks for reminding me. I'll get him out for the party. Is he going to be pissed, especially when he sees how much booze is left."

She makes a point of not watching you go behind her to the car. She doesn't want to see someone being humiliated. Plus also she needs to keep looking at me to be safe. I'm the one she doesn't trust.

I want to warn her, to tell her to run. I also just want things to be over.

You get the briefcase from the back seat. You don't completely shut the door, and you jiggle the keys as if you're about to open the trunk. Then you pretend to drop them and come sneaking over to us as quickly as you can.

You let go of the briefcase as soon as you get to her.

You take Adrian's hair into your hands. You have the knife. You tell me to take off all of my clothes. "Hurry up," you say. I do as I'm told.

I take the knife and hair. You undress, except for your underwear.

You grab the knife and cut Adrian's clothes off, taking a long long time.

You tell her how perfect she is as you cut. Better than you ever thought. She breathes through her nose like an excited horse. She stares at me. You pin her down, then tell me to open the briefcase. None of your fantasy girls are in there.

You take your underwear off. "Look at me," you say. "Look at me." It's starting to bother you that she doesn't, so you hit her. "Look at me." You just want Adrian to see how she makes you feel. She must understand that.

She looks then looks away.

She closes her eyes.

You tell her to suck you, and she does after a bit of a fight. You put it up the wrong end, she screams, then you shove it back into her mouth.

"Now who's my dirty girl?" you say.

She gags. Maybe she's going to be sick.

"Say you are my dirty girl." But she doesn't, even when you hit her, so you drop it. Things aren't working out. I can see you are pretty upset.

"I'm your dirty girl," I say, but you give me an ugly look, and I don't say anything more.

You tell Adrian and me to hug each other. I hug her. She keeps her arms limp. She plays dead. I don't mind. It's how I feel, too. A wave of love for her washes over me. She doesn't deserve this pain.

"Fuck off, Adrian," you say. "Do it."

You lick both our breasts after you ask us to squish them together and I've wiggled into the right position.

You tell us to kiss and then you put your penis between our lips.

You do Adrian from behind again while I'm lying pressed against her in front. I have to play with her down there while you do it. I have to lick her neck and breasts and face.

She is making choking sounds. She is trying to keep control. I see her tears tumble down, and I can't stand it.

Adrian is better than I'll ever be, and I can feel how much I hate her for it. Love her for it. Adrian and all the mean things she's said about you, she might as well have said how much better she is than me. And meanwhile, she's the one you really wanted—you've just barely put up with me, that's all.

Life really isn't fair. She's always going to remind me of that. Adrian is stronger than I'll ever be, and because of that, she'll die, I can feel it.

"Bastard," she says.

You tell her she's doing everything exactly like you want. You sound hurt. You take a vibrator from the briefcase and put it too far into her mouth. Then you put it almost everywhere. You take some twine and tie her up.

If she is a Jane, then every girl in the world is a Jane.

If she is a Jane, I'm less than a Jane.

She's too good to be treated this way. Things are going too far. I can see that something's going to happen. She looks at me.

Adrian is so sweet, even right at the end. I swear, she tells me she doesn't blame me for what is happening. I swear, she says she forgives me and that she feels sorry for me. She knows I have no choice.

You have your arm around her neck and slowly you tighten it. I have to pull away when she jerks around too much. Then she stops. You keep your arm there, just to make sure.

No, it's me. I have my hands on her. I do it. You try pulling my fingers from her throat, but you'd have to break them to get anywhere. I don't feel a thing, except my blood through my whole body. That's all I can hear, too, and the sound is pure—it tinkles, like a spring brook after the thaw. For once, what's happening to me seems to make sense, make everything clear. It's how I feel, underwater.

She shits herself, then dies. You are mad that I took her away too soon. You ask me why I had to do it. I ask you the same thing. We both know there isn't any answer. It's bigger than us.

After, you carry her like she is a bride going over the threshold. You are crying. I follow behind you with the knife. Our skin catches the moonlight through the trees.

We get to the creek and dunk her under a few times. The water is cold. I hold her in my arms. She feels so good. So at peace. I feel her spirit enter me. She thanks me. I want her body to be beautiful. I make sure that she is clean. I shake out her hair. I untie the nylons from her neck and let the water pull them away.

We are both so sad.

"You didn't have to do it," you say. "You did it too soon. Why did you do it at all?"

I hug her tight. I say, "She's mine."

You touch Adrian. You tell me, "I wasn't finished. You took her away before I was even finished."

"What are you talking about? You did everything." Sometimes you don't make any sense.

"Adrian, she's . . . I didn't really make her all mine."

"She's mine," I say. "She'll always be mine."

"You always had her. I just wanted her another way. You took that from me. Now she'll never really be a woman."

And then I finally figure it out. You were so busy doing the stuff that she obviously didn't like. Because you are so selfish. Except for the vibrator, Adrian is in actual fact still a virgin.

It's just too sad.

"Take her," I say. "Do it. It's not too late. She'll know."

I hand her over, and you pull her out of the river, and you do it. I get out of the water and watch. You kiss her. You tell her she is beautiful, and that you never meant to hurt her. That you love her in a special way. That you're sorry. I try to think of the last time you said words like those to me.

Then you bring her back. She is cold. I scrub at her down there. You were careful to come on her, not in her, and for that I am so grateful.

We take turns hugging her and kissing her on the lips. We say our goodbyes. We look at each other in a different way.

You go back and get some rope. I cut some of her hair for us to remember her by. We find two small, heavy boulders. Tie them around her neck and her thighs and put her under an overhanging rock, where the water is as deep as it gets. We put smaller rocks on her once she sinks, to cover her up.

Sometimes I can close my eyes and see her as she goes down, our Ophelia.

We wash ourselves off. Go to the car. Pick up everything we can find. Dress again, then drive to another place downstream a ways. The other girl comes out of the trunk, but I can see she's pretty far gone. Who knows what you've already done. I also notice for the first time that she's Chinese. Her head is bleeding, but you were careful to line the inside of the trunk with plastic.

We take her clothes off, put them beside her, and you fuck her a little, even though you don't seem very interested. She doesn't react. You say she's just like me on a good day, and I know it's supposed to hurt. You bite her ear, hard. You tell me to pee on her, and you pee on her, too. You put some things inside her.

Before, you said you found her especially for me. Actually, you used the word "it." I start kicking her, and you tell me to stop. I hurt my toe. Then I hold her and tell her I am sorry, that I don't know what came over me. I wouldn't have anything personal against a stranger. She is still pretty, in a way, and I give her some nice kisses all over to make up for it. The pee is kind of salty. I notice a tooth hanging loose in her mouth. I pull it when you're not looking, and put it into my own mouth. I tell her how much she is like me.

We aren't so careful with her. We wash her off. Put her under and throw as many rocks on her as we can. That's it. I'm not even sure if she is completely dead.

We rinse off. Get dressed again. Figure out where we should go. We go eat.

The next day, we burn all the clothes. It's easier for you, since I was in my best clothes while you were wearing crap. We go to an industrial park and dump the plastic lining. You take your car to a professional cleaners, telling your dad that it's having some kind of mechanical problem, so he lets you borrow the family junker for a few days.

You sell your car. You tell your dad it was too far gone to bother fixing. You use the junker for a few weeks, then get new wheels.

I don't tell you about the tooth, or about Adrian's purse with all her I.D., which I took from the back seat, or even about her hair.

A lot of times, I pop the tooth in my mouth and roll it around. This is weird, but it really helps calm me down.

# desire

I think about cutting myself. Taking broken glass to my wrists. Swallowing something sharp to slice up my insides. Putting the end of a knife against my heart and falling forward. For a while it's enough just to think about it, to wonder how it would feel, wonder what would be in my mind at the end. Imagine the guilt everyone would be saddled with. Where would I go, after?

Then I have to face up to the fact I could never actually do it. I'm just not strong enough. I get even more depressed. It feels like this emptiness will go on forever. I'm so pathetic.

After a while, I start to look through a catalogue and something catches my eye. Or else I just really get this feeling I need to shop. In a mall I'll be looking around, then I'll see some perfect thing, and my sadness is gone. I'll think, *I'll die if I don't get this*. I know that in the end I probably won't get it. But I'll think, *Someday*. It lets me think about the life I could have. The home I could make if I got the chance.

There will be another time for me, a different kind of life.

When I visited the doctor last week, I almost lost it. All of a sudden, there was this thing in my head of girls skipping. While the one jumped, the others sang:

*Passive, aggressive,*
*nar-sissy.*

139

*Do ya like t'fist-fuck?*
*You got ta tell me.*
*I said,*
*one, two, three, four . . .*


. . . that's the part where the girls turning count up till the one in the middle trips.

Which I never did when I was little. I only got bored and stopped. The doctor was asking me what I was thinking, but I didn't tell.

I'm not sure how to do this therapy thing yet. I've been reading a lot about psychology. I've been figuring it out. Nobody's going to trick me into saying what I don't want to.

When I was little, I went to church with my gran and gramps. I loved them very much, especially Grandpa. They kept me over every Sunday afternoon. Sometimes they gave me baths. They taught me right from wrong.

But then they died. They left me when I was still helpless and little, and needed them so much. Everything awful happened after they were gone. I guess I should at least try to be the girl my gran and gramps would have wanted. Fuckers.

I'm a girl and a girl never really decides anything, other than with make-up and fridges and shit. Anything else just happens. It's tricky, because sometimes I really believe I'm supposed to be more than all that. I'm so close to being bigger. And I'm definitely prettier than that sick bitch Rosemary West, and nicer. I'm smarter than the Florida hooker who whacked all those guys, and a lot younger. Plus, women don't normally use their hands. I read that.

I have to remember that it's not really my decision to make, and put this other stuff away, deep down inside. Who knows, maybe something else is going to happen, something else that'll make us count.

The future is what we make it.

# TWENTY

Early in the summer, I get work as a camp counsellor way up north. I really don't want the job, don't want to be so isolated, roughing it with a bunch of giggly thirteen-year-olds, but I take it because I need the money for when I leave home. An added bonus is that I won't have anywhere to spend it out there.

I haven't told anyone. The closer the time comes to leave, the more I regret that I'm going.

Weeks pass. The night before I'll be taking the bus to camp, we go out. I can't believe that I still haven't told you. At this point I'm kind of worried what you might do, what you might say when you find out. I'm worried you might get mad. It's not that I'm trying to keep a secret. I just don't want to go. I don't even want to talk about it. I block it out. My parents still don't know.

We take your car and park like we used to when we first started going out. I already feel far away from you. We talk about nothing. We make out. You call me your sweet girl, your baby. It's a really starry night. We can see the stars because we're outside of town.

Your hand rubs the inside of my thigh under my cut-offs, but I say, *Not now, it's almost my curfew.*

I know I'm hot there.

*Since when do you care about curfew?* You say it like you're talking to a four-year-old.

I know it's supposed to make me embarrassed, and make me want

141

you. But I've really got to go. I shouldn't be parking with you in the first place because the bus is leaving at quarter to six in the morning, and I still need to pack.

*Come on*, I keep saying, *I've really got to go.*

But it's like you can't even hear me. You keep pushing me to do what you want. What I want, too, I guess. We end up staying out all night.

When we're driving back, there's a narrow band of light stretched along the far end of town. The sky isn't black any more, but a deep, deep blue. The stars are still out, and the moon is full. It seems so huge, and it's riding above our car, over to the left and in front. I stare at it.

Then I say, *Look at the moon. Look at the moon.*

You look up and you say, *Fucking amazing. Look at that thing.*

The car keeps going, and the moon keeps sort of following it. The stars shift around. It's only a couple of seconds that we go on like this, but it seems like hours. Then you look down.

I'm still looking up when you say, *Holy fuck*, slam the brakes and swerve really sharp.

I can feel the muscles in my neck pull hard, my body snap back in answer to the car. I want to ask you what you're doing, but instead I'm ripped against the seat belt, straining away from the door. I look over and see my side of the car buckling, dull white metal flattening itself against the window, filling it. A spray of glass falls over me. Just as suddenly, we break away. My muscles are like concrete. I'm dizzy with fear.

I say, *What's happening, what's happening, what's happening?*

*It's a truck, a fucking truck parked at the edge of the fucking road. No lights or anything. Can you believe it? Can you fucking believe it?*

Your voice is fierce, but it also sounds like you're about to go through puberty again, like it's changing and you can't control it. You're trembling. Your hands are white against the wheel.

*Oh my god, oh my god*, I say.

*Wrecked the car for your fucking moon*, you say.

We don't pull over, and we don't talk about what just happened.

When we come to my parents' house, you stop and wait long enough for me to get out, then you take off. I feel bad that this will be our goodbye. There's a weak light all around now, and a few birds are starting to call. My key slides into the door. I press it gently counter-clockwise, trying to make sure that the tumblers inside don't make too much noise. Hoping not to wake anyone. I'm sure I'll find Mom or Dad on the La-Z-Boy, conked out after waiting up for me.

The door creaks and I die five hundred times. I feel sick. I close the door. I peek around the corner. There's no one there. I go to the kitchen to check the time. The bus for up north is going to leave in about ten minutes, and I haven't packed. There is no way I'm going to be ready. I can't think of any numbers to call.

I pack anyway, throwing in a dress, make-up and contact solution. I leave a little note on the kitchen counter.

I'm running as the morning gets stronger. My sneakers make a sharp wet sound on the dew-covered asphalt. A few dogs bark, and of course there are more birds out now, but still no people. I'm never up this early, so everything has a strange fresh look to it.

I get to where the bus should leave from. No one's there. Tread-marks cut their way across the damp surface of the road. I throw down my overnight bag. Standing still, I feel all the strain in my muscles from the accident. And I realize how stupid I am, how stupid this whole thing is. That I'm going, that I've missed the bus, that I've told no one, that I only have a dress with me.

I'm going into the woods, and I only have a dress with me.

That I looked at the moon.

Now I'm about to lose this job. The salt from my sweat is pulling at my skin, stinging my eyes. I've got to get in touch with the camp's senior counsellor. I have to explain.

At a pay phone, I call some number, then another, finally getting the right one for the camp from someone. When I call, the counsellor just says *Missus Workman* when she answers the phone.

I explain how I missed the bus, and how I've only got a dress with me and will need other clothes when I arrive.

She says that the next bus won't be for two weeks, and that those two weeks will be deducted from my pay.

*Of course,* I say. *Just thanks so much for letting me still work for you.*

There's no way at this point that I can get another summer job. And I guess it's too late for them to get someone else to replace me. So I wait, sitting at the stop. Somehow I manage to wait there the whole time.

My clothes are sticking to me when I arrive at the camp. I am desperate for a shower. The bus had been empty except for me and the driver, and after hours of quiet, the wall of excited noise from the girls comes as a shock. I've arrived just in time for some kind of bonding sport—a three-legged race or spoon-and-egg race or potato-sack race. They are squealing, grabbing each other, jumping around with so much energy it makes me more tired.

I hate girls this age. I'm only a few years older, but I feel like I've got nothing in common with them. I don't want to have anything in common. I can't remember ever running around, playing stupid games, giggling like an idiot. They must know what they look like. They must know what everyone thinks about them. I can't believe they don't care.

And behind all that ha-ha laughter they are all so mean and totally obsessed with themselves. What a horrible age. I don't believe girls like that grow out of it. They just learn to hide their stupid selves better. But they stay nasty, just thinking of themselves. Most girls, anyway.

I like my friends okay, but I still always watch it. Don't want to give them any information they could use against me later—throw my failures or weaknesses or doubts in my face. They're okay for shopping and, you know, talking about decorating and stuff, but anything personal, I keep it to myself.

Everything's so strange. Tents are all over. There is a tap on top of a pipe in the middle of the clearing where the girls play. I realize this is where the water comes from, and that the camp only has latrines. My contacts will be useless here.

There's a woman, she must be Missus Workman. She's in khaki shorts, a man's shirt, long blue socks, hiker boots, and she's wearing a funny little hat, like a boy scout's. She's lurking in the background, and doesn't seem to see me get off the bus. The girls keep scampering, keep giggling. Totally oblivious in their training bras.

One of the other counsellors, about my age, takes me for a tour of the grounds. Trees and more trees. Bugs. We get to a pretty isolated spot. *Wait here*, she says.

It's not too long before she's back. She's talking, but I can't really hear what she's saying. It's garbled. The gist of it is that Missus Workman thinks I owe her for being so late. I have to make up for it by doing a good deed.

What comes out clear is my co-worker saying, *You've got to show you're responsible, 'cause you're going to be responsible for all these girls up here.*

I ask what I should do about my clothes.

*We've scavenged around to get you some things*, she says. *You'll be okay. But you know, she wants you to make up for this. She wants you to be responsible.*

I notice we've stopped in another little clearing. I hadn't realized we were walking. She tells me this is where the camp's mascot is kept. Missus Workman and a couple of the girls arrive. I start to get the same uneasy feeling in my stomach that I had once in grade three. I'd squeezed an orange on a teacher's tree even though we'd been told not to touch. As my hand pulled back through the window, another teacher at the other end of the open-concept room looked up and saw me. I spent the rest of recess knowing I was going to be spanked in front of sixty kids. I kept telling Adrian that I was going to be sick (I wasn't). She tried to convince me that the teacher didn't see me. She was wrong. I was spanked. So was Adrian, because the teacher saw her beside me, and the rules were she should have reported me.

I feel sick like that now. But all I have to do is take care of the camp mascot overnight. Keep it warm. No big deal.

By this time, it's mid-afternoon. Everything is dry and crisp. There's the sound of insects rubbing their legs. The hum of a motor boat far away. Wind through the trees. I feel my hair swirl with the wind, pulling at the back of my head when there's a big gust. Sometimes the ends of a few strands snap across my face, stinging my eyes.

I shift from foot to foot. I notice how much paler my legs are compared to the other girls'. One of the kids has gone to get the mascot. It's as if the sun is being pulled down by its own weight, against its will.

The others don't meet my eyes.

When she gets back, the girl is carrying a huge snake—a boa constrictor. It is placed in front of my feet, where it doesn't move. Missus Workman comes to me. *Make sure it doesn't die,* she says. *You have to keep it warm. Do anything for it.*

She sounds bitter. Hateful. She walks away. Everyone else follows behind. I am alone with the snake, neither of us moving for hours.

In the early evening, the air begins to cool. If it's possible, the snake looks even more still than before. The sun is so heavy in the sky, it won't be there for much longer. And it dawns on me—a growing understanding that becomes more clear, then seems so obvious. I'm going to have to keep this snake warm overnight. That's my job. The panicky sick feeling comes back into my gut. A boa constrictor kills its prey by crushing the air out of it. That was in a documentary one time. I can't wrap it around me for body heat. I don't know how to start a fire.

This is just so crazy.

A foot, then a hand, brushes against the snake's body. It doesn't stir. I have to act fast. I pick up the snake just behind its head and start pushing it into my mouth. It is surprisingly limp and easy to handle as I coil it inside.

The pressure is incredible, but the snake manages to fit. My jaws feel like they might break. I think of that old TV show where the aliens pretended to be human but really looked like lizards. I must look like that—my jaws wide apart just before I drop a rat into them. I have the same kind of choking tension I get at the dentist just before I can spit. Swallow. No, don't swallow.

The trick is not to move. Maybe the snake will do the same. My back is against a tree, my arms limp at my sides. I fight the need to gag. My throat tightens, relaxes, tightens, relaxes. I try to name the changing colours in the sky. Try to watch the movements of the stars and satellites. It works for a while.

I've been dozing, but I suddenly wake up about an hour before the sun is going to come up. It's as though I had a falling dream and came to before hitting bottom, but then there is a hard push at the back of my throat. That's what must have broken my sleep. The snake must be too cramped, and it's figured out that there is more space down there. Inside me.

I'm coughing. This does not stop the snake. Instead, it uses the muscle spasms to get its head in more. If I don't die from the snake going down me, I could die from having puke rush up and go nowhere. Then I'd breathe it into my lungs. I can't remember what that's called. There is no time to think.

Get the snake out. There's no point being mad at it. It's only trying to get comfortable. This is nothing against me personally. But I've got to get it out. I open my lips, grab its tail, and pull gently. It coils tighter into my mouth. Jabs hard into the back of my throat. I can feel the head pushing down the inside of my neck. It must be scared.

I panic. Start grabbing at anything in there. Everything's so slippery, but finally my nails dig into flesh and pull something back. Even so, I can feel the pressure—the snake is still in there, pushing. I had thought that once I got something solid, the whole snake would come with it—that it would try to not get hurt. Now I figure that it's stuck and can only go forward, down me.

So I grab at it like a maniac. By this time I just want it out. It must be terrible for the snake. I'm tearing off chunks of it. This is so bad. I love animals. A sharp acid taste washes over my mouth in bursts. This is just too awful. There is now enough room to start spitting, which I do. I get the snake out, but the taste stays. I keep spitting.

There is no question, the snake is dead. I hate myself. Its eyes are open and glassy. Its body is more or less together, but pieces are scattered around me. There's nothing left to do except sit and wait for the others to find what I've done.

Give me a kiss to build a dream on,
And my imagination will thrive upon that kiss.
Sweetheart I ask no more than this,
A kiss to build a dream on.

Give me a kiss before you leave me,
And my imagination
Will feed my hungry heart.
Leave me one thing before we part,
A kiss to build a dream on.

When I'm alone
With my fantasies
I'll be with you
Weaving romances
Making believe they're true.

Give me your lips for just a moment,
And my imagination
Will make that moment live.
Give me what you alone can give,
A kiss to build a dream on.

# ACKNOWLEDGEMENTS

For convincing me there was a story to tell (and that I could tell it), my thanks go to David Hunt and Rick Salutin.

The Potentially Publishable Women's Literary Group—Nadine Leggette, Virginia Mak, Suzanne Methot, Hazelle Palmer and Barb Thomas—was instrumental to the direction of the book.

Lisa Germano kept me constant company as I wrote. Her musical exploration of some of the same terrain I was travelling provided powerful support and affirmation. I cannot thank her enough.

Nelson Ball, Barbara Caruso, Daniel Hall, Charlotte Montgomery, Ian Pearson, Kam Rao, Stuart Ross, Ann Shin, Iris Tupholme and Eddy Yanofsky were wonderful critical readers who gracefully put up with my endless talk about the manuscript.

There are many other people who spent hours in conversation with me about the book over the past six years. While I won't name each of you here, I do want you all to know your contributions are appreciated.

The final stretch was made possible by my family, Friend's House, Karma Co-op, Elaine McNinch, as well as Mike Constable, Shelly Cope, Kundra Fotheringham and the other folks at Naivelt.

Brian Lam and Blaine Kyllo of Arsenal Pulp, and Beverley Daurio and Don Daurio of The Mercury Press have been great to work with. I remain surprised and delighted that an off-the-wall suggestion to publish *Jane* together was greeted with enthusiasm by both presses.

Hats off to Barbara Klunder and Joan Hutton for their superb artwork.

Finally, this writer would like to thank the Ontario Arts Council, and by extension the people of that province, for a Writers' Reserve grant received early on in the book's development.

—J.M.